Also by Jane Peart

Orphan Train West for Young Adults
    Toddy
    Kit
    Ivy and Allison
    April and May

Edgecliffe Manor Mysteries
    Web of Deception
    Shadow of Fear
    A Perilous Bargain
    Thread of Suspicion

Laurel

Jane Peart

Fleming H. Revell
A Division of Baker Book House Co
Grand Rapids, Michigan 49516

Published by Fleming H. Revell
a division of Baker Book House Company
P.O. Box 6287, Grand Rapids, MI 49516-6287

Adapted from *Quest for Lasting Love,* published in 1990

Second printing, April 2001

Printed in the United States of America

Library of Congress Cataloging-in Publication Data

Peart, Jane.
    Laurel / Jane Peart.
       p. cm.
    "Adapted from Quest for lasting love published in 1990"—T.p. verso.
    Summary: Although she had been adopted by a loving couple following her mother's death, Laurel searches for her biological roots before finally finding her "real" home.
    ISBN 0-8007-5713-0 (paper)
    [1. Orphans—Fiction. 2. Family life—Fiction. 3. Christian life—Fiction.] I. Peart, Jane. Quest for lasting love. II. Title.
PZ7.P32334 Lau 2000
[Fic]—dc21   99-044201

Scripture quotation is from the King James Version of the Bible.

For current information about all releases from Baker Book House, visit our web site:

http://www.bakerbooks.com

Boston 1888

Something dreadful was about to happen. Laurel just knew it. Mama had seemed strange all morning. In fact, Mama had not seemed like herself for weeks. Day by day, the six-year-old could feel the little knot in her chest grow tighter. Something was wrong.

Laurel's mother, Lillian Vestal, gave piano lessons on Tuesday and Thursday afternoons in Mrs. Campbell's boardinghouse where they lived. The little girl always played quietly in a corner of the room while the students fumbled through their scales and simple pieces. Usually after the last pupil had left, Lillian would sit at the piano and play lovely melodies, filling the room with music. Many times they would sing songs together. Laurel loved singing with her mother. However, lately they hadn't even been doing that. Instead, her mother had been closing the piano lid with a deep sigh. Then, pale and exhausted, she would lie down on the narrow sofa, one arm flung over her eyes.

Several nights over the past few weeks, Laurel had awakened to her mother's footsteps on the hardwood floor, the sound of a hoarse racking cough trailing her mother down the hallway to the living room. Frightened, Laurel would hug her doll, Miranda. On these nights, Laurel lay in her small bed thinking about how much she loved her mother.

They did everything together. At mealtimes the two would pretend that their simple fare of bread, tea with milk, and fruit was a gala affair fit for royalty. Many times her mother would play games with her. Laurel would be Princess Laura Elaine, her real christened name after the two faraway grandmothers whom she had never met.

"You'll meet them one day," her mother often promised, "when all is forgiven." Laurel didn't know exactly what this meant, but she was so happy with the life she and her mother had together that she did not trouble herself about it.

On this particular morning, Laurel heard the steady pattering of a November rain against the windows. Before she was fully awake, she felt her mother's hand gently stroking her hair.

"Come, darling, you must get up."

Laurel sat up, sleepily rubbing her eyes. "Is it night-time?" she asked, watching her mother's slender figure in her drifting white nightgown move about in the lamplight, setting their small table for breakfast.

"No, precious, it's very early in the morning. But we have somewhere to go, so I'm fixing a special breakfast for us. Cocoa for you and a special surprise: sticky buns!"

An uneasy sensation stirred within her. Something in her mother's tone didn't seem right.

After they had eaten, her mother brushed Laurel's curly, dark brown hair.

"You know, darling, Mama hasn't been feeling well lately," she said as she carefully wound each curl around her thin fingers, tying one bunch of hair with a blue velvet ribbon. "The doctor says I must go away to a place in the mountains where some people can take care of me so I can get strong again. While I'm gone, you're going to stay at a nice place with a lot of other little girls and boys—"

"But I don't want to go anywhere without you, Mama!"

"I know, darling, but it'll only be for a little while. I'll come to get you as soon as I can." Her mother's voice shook as she hugged her. The child felt the wetness of tears flowing down her mother's soft cheek. She clung to her mother in panic.

Laurel watched her mother pack a small valise with her neatly ironed clothes all handmade by Lillian. Laurel loved the embroidered, lace-trimmed dresses and ruffled petticoats.

Then her mother unclasped the gold chain holding the locket she always wore around her own neck and fastened it around Laurel's.

"I want you to wear this until I come for you, Laurel." She pointed out the swirled letters on the heart-shaped front. "See these? They spell our initials. The L.M. stands for Lillian Maynard, my maiden name. The P.V. is for your father, Paul Vestal. He gave me this before we were married."

Her mother opened the locket to show her the pictures inside. One was Lillian when she was a young girl, her dark hair falling in curls around her shoulders. The other was Laurel's father, a dark-eyed handsome young artist, tragically killed by a team of runaway horses as he was crossing the street. Laurel was too little to remember him, but she loved the beautiful landscape he had painted of a lighthouse on a beach. Her mother had hung it over the piano where everyone could see it.

"Now remember, Laurel, don't take this off until I come to get you."

Her mother buttoned the handmade, blue velour coat with its scalloped cape. After tying Laurel's satin bonnet strings under her chin, she kissed her on both cheeks. Then, hand in hand, the two walked quietly down the stairs of the sleeping house and out into the dark, rainy Boston morning.

At the street corner, they found a cab and sad-looking horse, its driver bundled in a wool muffler. Lillian squeezed her daughter's hand. "This is going to be an adventure, darling."

"Where to, lady?" the driver asked.

"Greystone." Lillian helped Laurel mount the high, rickety steps into the cab.

"You mean the County Orphanage?" he asked.

"Yes," Lillian's voice quavered.

Inside, she put her arm around Laurel, drawing her close. The ancient buggy swayed and jolted over the cobblestone streets, jogging slowly up a steep hill. Laurel felt the chill creep through the cracks of the old vehicle into her bones. She shivered and leaned into her mother. Finally, the cab jerked to a stop in front of a giant stone building.

The driver opened the roof flap and announced, "Grey-stone!"

Lillian lifted Laurel down. Then she said to the cabby, "Wait, please, I need a ride to the train depot."

Holding one of Laurel's hands, she mounted the steps. At the massive double door, she twisted the metal door-bell. A tall woman with little half glasses that cut across her thin nose opened the door.

"Yes?"

"I'm Lillian Vestal." Her mother's voice was faint. "This is my daughter."

"Ah, yes, Mrs. Vestal. We were expecting you." The woman stretched out a bony hand toward Laurel, who drew back. "It's best you leave now, ma'am. There'll be less of a fuss if you say good-bye here."

When her mother bent down to hug her, Laurel wrapped her little hands around her neck. She didn't understand what was happening.

"You must be a brave, good girl, my darling," her mother whispered. "I'll be back soon. Very soon."

Lillian pried her daughter's hands from around her neck. The next thing the little girl knew she was being pulled out of her mother's embrace and picked up by the stranger.

"Mama! Mama!" Laurel screamed as her mother started down the steps. "Come back!"

Then, all of a sudden, the big door slammed shut behind her.

The third floor dormitory was a long room lined with rows of small iron cots. Beside each bed was a small chest with an enamel pitcher, a washbowl, and a wooden stool. As Miss Clinock entered with Laurel, two dozen heads turned sharply.

"Get on with your duties, children." The head matron's order was crisp. "Come along, Laurel," she said as she led the youngster toward an unmade narrow cot.

"Kit," Miss Clinock addressed a girl with smooth brown braids who was pulling up the covers of her own cot next to Laurel's. "Will you please show Laurel how to make her bed and put her clothes neatly away?"

"Yes, ma'am," the girl answered shyly.

For the first three days, Laurel got up, put on her blue velour coat with its short cape and matching bonnet, went down the main stairway, and planted herself on the bottom step. "My mother's coming to get me," she stated flatly, her arms folded across her chest.

"Laurel, your mother left you with us while she's in the sanatorium getting well." The tall head matron towered over her. "Until then, she expects you to be obedient and do as you're told. Now, come along." Miss Clinock held out her hand. "You want us to give your mother a good report when she does come, don't you? So while you're at Greystone, you'll wear what the other children wear. We'll put away the things your mother made for you so they'll be ready when she comes."

Tears turned Laurel's eyes into glistening coals. She didn't want Mama to be disappointed in her. Slowly she got up, lifted her chin bravely, and followed Miss Clinock to the sewing room to get a uniform.

That night, the little girl planted her head in her pillow and cried softly. If only she hadn't left her doll at the apartment. If only she had Miranda to cuddle.

"I know how you feel." The voice was Kit Ternan's. "I felt the same way when I first came here."

"But I'm not going to stay here." Laurel fingered the delicate chain of the locket still hanging around her neck and squeezed her eyes shut, letting more tears flow. "My mother's coming for me."

"So is mine."

Laurel opened her eyes to see a smiling face and round blue eyes staring at her.

"My name is Victorine Zephronia Todd," she added proudly, "but you can call me Toddy. My mother's in France, and she's coming back to get me too. Any day now." The girl plopped herself down on the bed beside Laurel.

"So's my Da," Kit added, gently stroking Laurel's dark curls. "At least, as soon as he gets a job."

No three girls were more different in appearance or personality, yet an immediate bond was formed. Laurel, Kit, and Toddy became inseparable as the weeks turned into months. The three sat at the same table at mealtimes and played together during recreation. Since their cots were side by side in the dormitory, they often sought out one another during the long, lonely nights.

After the first week, Laurel received a letter enclosing a picture of the sanatorium from her mother. "This is where I sit in the fresh air every day," it read. "I miss you very much. Soon we'll be together again, my darling."

The little girl printed letters to her mother. Because daisies were her mother's favorite flowers, she carefully drew them down the border of the page and on the flap of the envelope. Miss Clinock mailed them for her.

One day in Laurel's fourth week at Greystone, Miss Clinock sent for her to come to her office, a long room with a high ceiling.

"Sit down, Laurel, I have something to tell you."

Laurel noticed two envelopes in the head matron's hands. She immediately recognized the daisies on the back flap. They had to be the last two letters she had sent to her mother!

"Do you know what this word means, Laurel?" Miss Clinock showed her a big black word marked on the front of each envelope. It said D-E-C-E-A-S-E-D.

Laurel's heart began a drumbeat that felt as if her chest was exploding. "No, ma'am," she replied in a hoarse whisper.

"It says 'deceased,' Laurel. The word means that your mother is dead."

She sat there, glued to the straight chair opposite Miss Clinock's desk. *Dead?* The six-year-old did not know what *dead* was. The lady who owned the boardinghouse had a cat that had died. And Laurel knew her father was in heaven. But what was *dead?*

"Are you all right, Laurel?" prompted the head matron. "Do you understand what I just told you?"

Somehow the next few days passed by like a gray fog. Toddy and Kit stayed close by, but Laurel still felt alone. Her mother was never coming back. She was alone in the world. Now she knew how the other children felt. She had become just like them: an orphan.

Meadowridge

Located in a quiet, peaceful valley, the town of Meadowridge, Arkansas, was bordered by rolling hills and a long, winding river. Its grazing cattle, pleasant houses, and well-kept yards were a far cry from the rowdy mining town it had once been.

Dr. Leland Woodward parked his small black buggy in the cleared area between the Meadowridge Community Church and the large pasture. He sat for a minute, the reins slack in his hands, listening to the singing voices floating out from inside the white frame building. He was late for the eleven o'clock Sunday service, but he'd had to go home first to bathe, shave, and change. The well-liked doctor had been out most of the night delivering a baby.

Leland ran his hand through his thick hair, just turning gray at the temples as he neared forty. He reached for his felt hat on the seat beside him, put it on, gave the gray brim a snap, and got down from the buggy. Then he tethered the mare to a nearby maple tree, close enough to the fence so she could reach over and nibble some of the early spring grass in the meadow. Mounting the church steps, the tall, handsome man walked inside.

Leland sighed as he sat down in an empty spot. He and Ava used to have a regular pew in the church every Sunday. But his wife didn't attend church much nowadays. In fact, she scarcely left the house at all anymore. Folks seemed to understand, and yet it was already 1890. Two years was a long time.

The doctor had just slipped into a back pew when he heard Pastor Brewster announce a guest speaker. "Let us welcome Rev. Matthew Scott to our church today. We're honored to have him come to us all the way from the Christian Rescuers and Providers' Society in Boston."

A tall, thin young man with rusty-brown hair and wire-rimmed glasses stepped up to the lectern.

"Thank you, Pastor Brewster. Ladies and gentlemen, I've spent two days in your town and the surrounding countryside," he began. "I've walked your shady streets and driven by your neat farmhouses along the hillsides. I've seen evidence of prosperity and contentment everywhere."

The speaker's voice was rich and full. Dr. Woodward settled himself comfortably on the seat as he listened.

"Picture, if you will, a dingy flat in the city where a dying single mother lies in a bed covered by a threadbare blanket while her children hover around a cold stove. Or an abandoned seven-year-old digging in the garbage in an alley, looking for food during the freezing cold of a New England winter.

"In the past five years, the Rescuers and Providers' Society has been actively involved in rescuing children like these and bringing them by train to places such as Meadowridge here in the West. Our main goal is to provide these lost children with Christian homes so they can be trained up to become God-fearing, law-abiding citizens. It grieves me greatly even to mention the alternative that awaits them, a life lived on the streets and possibly one of crime."

Leland swallowed hard. Although he rarely showed his emotions, something in this man's words caused his throat to tighten.

It had been two years since the death of his seven-year-old daughter. The question that sometimes tortured him came to his mind. Had he brought the diphtheria virus home during the epidemic? Leland quickly shook his head in an attempt to make the thoughts go away and concentrate on what the speaker was saying.

"Because of this, I am encouraged today to ask you this question. You, who live in these bountiful circum-stances," the speaker's arm moved in a wide circle as he spoke, "will you take one of these unfortunate chil-dren into your home, to raise in a healthy Christian atmosphere?"

The soft sound of muffled sniffles echoed through the sanctuary. The visiting pastor took off his glasses and wiped his own eyes before continuing.

"If any of you feel led to offer your home, my wife and I will be here for the next few days. We'll be more than happy to answer your questions."

Before Pastor Scott had finished, the doctor knew his heart had been touched. After the last hymn, he sat a few moments before leaving, wondering if he dared sug-gest such a thing? What would Ava say?

Leland thought about the charming girl he had married, her laughing hazel eyes and sparkling smile. He missed her so. Ever since the loss of Dorie, nothing had been the same. His wife suffered from a depression so deep nothing seemed to be able to lift the dark cloud of sorrow from her. She had kept Dorie's room untouched. Their daughter's dolls, toys, playthings, and books remained as though she might come running in from school at any minute.

Her husband knew this was unhealthy. Everything should be put away, given away, swept out of sight. Leaving things like this only kept his grieving wife moored in the same desperate state of sadness. Here he was, a man of medicine who brought healing to others, helpless to help the one he loved so dearly.

Oh, how he missed the sound of a child's voice and running feet on the stairs. His father's heart yearned for the laughter and excitement only children could bring. Yes, maybe he would pursue the thought, but he would wait until just before the Orphan Train was due to press Ava for a decision.

He left the church and walked over to join the cluster of people waiting to meet Rev. Scott. He hesitated. Better not say anything right away. No, he would pray about it and seek God's will in the matter. In the meantime, he would gently persuade his wife at least to start thinking about it. Ava had always loved children. She was made to be a mother. Leland would pray that her gentle, caring heart was still there, able to love another.

The Orphan Train

Laurel saw her face reflected in the train window as if in a mirror. She stared out into the darkness as the Orphan Train sped across the prairie through the night.

Like the others, she'd been given a small cardboard suitcase in which to pack her few belongings for the long trip. To her dismay, she discovered she had outgrown the beautiful clothes her mother had made for her, so she had to accept the plain blue dress and pinafores, warm coat and bonnet Miss Clinock gave the girls for the journey. Laurel moved, shifting her position on the hard coach seat. Unconsciously, her hand moved to her neck, fingering the chain and locket with her parents' pictures. The little girl had promised Mama she would never take it off. Now, all she had left of her life before Greystone was this locket.

With her finger, the seven-year-old began to spell out her name on the gritty surface of the windowsill. "LAUREL VESTAL."

As she wrote, she formed the words silently with her tongue: "My name is Laurel Vestal." The metallic clickety-clack of the train wheels along the steel rails seemed to repeat them. *Laurel Vestal. Laurel Vestal.*

Laurel closed her eyes and wished the old wish that would never come true. She tried to wish herself back to the little flat in Boston on the top floor of Mrs. Campbell's boardinghouse, tried to hear her mother playing the piano, tried to recall the melodies of her favorite music.

The little girl blinked, trying not to cry. Why had her mother not told her the truth about how sick she was and that she might die? The tears rolled down one by one now, forming sooty streaks on her rosy cheeks. Laurel could not stop them.

Just then the mournful sound of the train whistle hooted shrilly as the locomotive approached a crossing. Laurel huddled further into the skimpy blanket and pressed her face against the window. She liked it when the train slowed down as it went through small towns where she could see little, yellow square lights in the houses they passed. Maybe a mother was knitting inside and children were playing on the floor. Maybe a father was reading a fairy tale to his children. The familiar longing gripped her heart. The emptiness she felt just wouldn't go away.

The day after tomorrow they would be in Meadowridge, the last stop on the trip. Mrs. Scott had shown them where it was on the map she had pinned up on the wall. She said it was the most pleasant town she had ever seen, that she would like to live there herself.

Laurel's eyes began to feel heavy. She was sleepy. She pushed the lumpy pillow under her head and closed her eyes. Toddy was asleep right beside her, her riotous red curls covering her pillow. Laurel was glad she had listened to Toddy's secret plan, even though the trio had gotten in trouble for it. It had been like a game and it was the only way they could be sure they wouldn't be separated.

She smiled. Kit had dragged her leg as if she were crippled. And Toddy had looked so funny with her eyes crossed and her face twisted in the most awful expression. Laurel had hiked one shoulder higher than the other when she walked. The charade had worked at each stop. No one had wanted to adopt the three unsightly children.

On the morning of the Orphan Train's arrival, Leland Woodward stopped at the door of his wife's darkened sitting room. "It's a beautiful spring day, my dear. Why are the shutters closed and the curtains drawn? Let me open them to let in some of this lovely sunshine."

"No, please, Lee," she protested, raising a fragile hand. "I have a slight headache. The glare bothers my eyes."

Leland walked over to the flowered chaise lounge where Ava Woodward lay. "Do you think you'll feel better later, well enough to go with me to the train station? It's due at one o'clock."

"Oh, no, Lee, I couldn't." Ava shook her head.

"But the child—don't you want to help me choose?"

"No," she murmured. "It was your decision."

"But we discussed it thoroughly, my dear, and you agreed." Leland stopped an impulse to get irritated.

"Because you want it so, Leland." Ava sighed. "You can be very persuasive."

Leland clenched his fists. "Ava, if you had any doubts about this, you should have expressed them when I first brought up the subject. The children are on their way now."

Ava's fingers picked at the fringe of the blue shawl wrapped around her thin shoulders. She did not meet his pleading eyes. "I've had a room made ready," she said meekly. "Be patient with me, Lee. It'll take time."

"It's been two years, dear. It's time we got on with our lives." He paused. "A child is what this house needs now. You said so yourself."

"I know, Lee. I thought I was ready. But now I don't know."

The doctor pulled his watch out of his vest pocket and looked at it. "I have to make a few house calls. I'll be back by noon. Please make the effort to come with me to the train. It would mean a great deal to me. And to the child."

He leaned down and kissed her cheek then left the room. Maybe it had been a mistake to talk his wife into taking one of the Orphan Train children. A terrible mistake. Yet, down deep he didn't think so. He felt it was the right thing to do. Leland had written the Scotts that he and his wife would take a little boy into their home. A boy would be easier for Ava to accept than a little girl. The doctor liked the idea of a son, a child people might call "Doc's boy."

At twenty minutes before one o'clock, Dr. Woodward arrived at the Meadowridge Church hall, alone. His wife had not come with him. Since he had volunteered to give the children a brief physical checkup, he busily set up a makeshift office. He filled a glass tumbler with wooden tongue depressors and adjusted the window blind for more light.

His mind was still troubled. What should he do now? Suppose Ava really did not want a child. Perhaps he could explain to the Scotts—

Suddenly, the door of the social hall opened with a burst of people. Soon the town doctor was busy peering down little throats, checking ears, and listening to the thrumming of dozens of healthy little hearts.

He was just finishing some paperwork when he looked up to greet his last patient. When he did, long-lashed brown eyes regarded him steadily, a tiny smile tugging at the rosebud mouth. Tendrils of dark hair curled around a rosy face and fell in beautiful curls onto her shoulders. She was the prettiest little girl he had seen that day.

The doctor held out both hands. "Well, little lady, come in. Don't be afraid. I won't hurt you. What's your name?"

"Laurel," she replied, approaching him slowly.

Before looking down her throat, the doctor allowed the little girl to hold the tongue depressor. He let her listen to his chest and hear his heartbeat before placing the stethoscope on her heart.

The more he gazed into her sweet little face and saw her smile, the more convinced he became that this was the child they were meant to have. Why, the child even laughed at his silly jokes! Slowly but surely the conviction grew within him that this child, a girl, would bring with her the blessing he had been praying for since that day Matthew Scott had spoken at the church. God had heard his prayers. With this child, the Lord would restore the joy that had been missing in the Woodward household for too long.

The doctor leaned forward and took both of Laurel's little hands in his.

"Laurel, would you like to come home with me and be my little girl?" His big eyes almost pleaded. "We have a big backyard with trees and a swing, and there's even a pond with goldfish swimming in it. I think you would like it."

Laurel looked into the strong face searching hers. Behind his glasses, kindly blue eyes twinkled. She could feel the warmth.

"Well, Laurel, what do you say?"

"Yes." She nodded solemnly.

Leland's heart swelled. He took out his handkerchief to wipe the mist on his glasses. Then, clearing his throat, he said, "Come on then, let's make it official."

Within a few minutes, Leland was lifting his new daughter up into his buggy and placing her small suitcase on the floor in front of her so she could put her feet on it. "Well, Laurel, we're off. We're going home."

Home. The word made Laurel feel excited but at the same time a little afraid. Home had always meant the cozy little rooms on top of Mrs. Campbell's house with Mama. She still missed her mama so much. The deep feelings of sadness swept over her again.

The horse trotted across an arched stone bridge leading up a main street. Weeping willows lined the sloping banks of a winding river. Then they turned onto a pleasant curving street lined with shade trees. Neat houses were set back from the road with pretty gardens behind picket fences. They slowed to a halt, and the horse stopped in front of a white frame house. The doctor didn't even have to say, "Whoa."

The house had lace curtains at green shuttered windows. Baskets of pink geraniums swung along the railings at the top of the deep porch. It looked nice and friendly.

"Are you hungry?" the doctor asked as he helped her down and took her hand.

Laurel shook her head. "No, thank you," she answered politely.

"Well, I am, and thirsty too! I'll tell you what. We'll go into the kitchen and see if Ella, our cook, has some lemonade and maybe some cookies." He led her up the steps. "Then we'll go upstairs so you can meet my wife. Come on."

A few minutes later, Leland left Laurel swinging on the front porch swing eating a warm oatmeal cookie while he went uptsairs to tell Ava what he had done. He found her still lying on the chaise in her sitting room.

Ava Woodward stared at her husband. "Oh, Lee, how could you? Bringing a little girl into this house. She can never take Dorie's place!"

"She's not intended to take Dorie's place, Ava," Leland replied kindly. "No one could do that." The doctor sat down beside her on the soft cushion. "She'll make her own place here. Give her time. Give yourself time to get to know her."

"You said you were getting a boy, and I agreed to that." She clasped her thin hands together. "You know how I longed to give you a son of your own." Ava closed her eyes. "But this . . . you're asking too much, Leland."

"Darling, I would never knowingly hurt you," he replied, hope trickling out of his heart.

When he leaned forward to kiss her, she held up her hand to ward him off. The silence that followed stretched between them. The doctor stood up, walked to the door, and closed it quietly behind him.

The next few days Ava Woodward maintained a cold silence toward her husband. It seemed a terrible breach of trust for him to bring a little girl into their lives again. It was creating a chasm wider and more dangerous than any they had ever faced in their fifteen-year marriage.

Since Dorie's death, Ava had not come downstairs for breakfast. Most nights, she couldn't sleep. Since Laurel's coming, she stayed in bed until she heard Leland leave the house to go on his house calls every morning. Then she shut herself up in her sitting room.

On the third morning, Ava rose and stood at the door. Leland was speaking to someone downstairs. Hearing the front door close, she lifted her shaking hands to her throbbing temples. Her head hurt again. She knew the signs—shooting flashes of light, dizziness, clammy palms. Getting upset always brought on one of her headaches.

She pressed her fingers over her eyes for a minute. Dear God, what should she do? She dearly loved her husband and she wanted him to be happy. But she couldn't do this!

Ava walked over to a window overlooking the garden out back. Pushing the flowered curtain aside, she looked down and saw Leland, hand in hand with the little girl, walking along the flagstone path to the gate leading to the stable. She watched as he bent down, one hand gently stroking the child's long, dark curls as he talked to her. Then he kissed her cheek and went through the gate. The youngster jumped on the bottom ledge, leaning over the top and waving her hand. For a few minutes the child stayed there, swinging back and forth on the open gate. As the sounds of the horse's hooves and buggy wheels died away, she got down, turned, and walked back through the garden.

In spite of herself, Ava's heart was touched at the sight of the lonely small figure in the drab denim dress and pinafore. Suddenly the stabbing pain in her head made Ava sway slightly. She grabbed onto the nearby chair to steady herself, then she stumbled over to lie down on the chaise lounge.

Laurel sat on the bottom step of the polished staircase. The house was hushed. There was not a sound anywhere. Today, Dr. Lee had gone out on house calls. Both Ella and Jenny Appleton, the Woodwards' maid, had the day off.

Laurel sighed. She was lonely. She was glad to be in this lovely big house with the doctor, but she missed Kit and Toddy. The doctor had promised she could have them over to play in a few weeks, but a few weeks was a long time to wait. Today, she had an entire afternoon in front of her with nothing to do.

Laurel had met Mrs. Woodward only once, the night she arrived. Laurel thought she was pretty but very pale. The doctor told her his wife was sick. However, while she was waiting in the hall for the doctor to come out, she had overheard Mrs. Woodward say, "Lee, why in the world did you bring that child here?"

The thought caused a sad little ache to press against Laurel's chest. Mrs. Woodward did not want her. What was going to happen to her? Would she be placed out somewhere else?

There was nothing much for a girl to play with here either. The room she stayed in had been prepared for a boy, with lots of books about Indians, a building game, and a set of toy soldiers. Laurel would have liked paper dolls to cut out or jackstraws or a book of fairy tales.

Just like she did every night before bed, she took out her locket, flipped it open, and kissed the two oval pictures. She missed her mama so much at times she could hardly stand it. She couldn't let the memories fade. But two long years had passed, and so much had happened. The little girl crossed her arms and hugged herself, rocking back and forth.

With nothing else to do, Laurel scooted up the stairs. She counted the rungs of the stair railings on each step as she went. Humming a little tune her mother had taught her, the youngster slowly moved from step to step until she finally reached the top of the stairway.

Holding the oak banister, she pulled herself to her feet. Her first impulse was to mount it and slide backward down its smooth, satiny surface. Instead, she decided to go search for an interesting picture book in her room. Then she could take it outside and sit in the porch swing until Dr. Lee came home.

However, as she started down the hallway, she noticed a door. It was cracked open. This door had always been closed before. Curious, she moved closer and peered in. Nobody was inside. She pushed the door open.

Sun poured in through crisp, white, ruffled curtains onto the flowered cushions of the window seat. A big doll with blond curls sat in a small wicker chair by a low table all set with little dishes. Under the window were shelves full of toys, games, and books.

Wide-eyed and full of wonder, Laurel stepped in. She walked very slowly as if in a dream. It was a little girl's room, and what a wonderful room it was! A scrolled white iron bed with a ruffled cover was piled high with dolls and stuffed animals. A tiny red rocking chair in one corner was decorated with painted flowers.

And then her eyes spotted the most thrilling thing of all: a large peaked-roof dollhouse. Laurel tiptoed over to it and knelt down in front to peer into the tiny rooms. There was a parlor, a bedroom, and a little nursery with a bassinet and tiny china baby doll. There was even a kitchen with wee little pots and pans. Laurel put out her hand to move one of the dolls that had fallen out of the winged chair next to the fireplace.

"Don't touch that!"

Startled, she jerked around and dropped the little figure. Mrs. Woodward was standing in the doorway. Masses of dark hair tumbled wildly around her shoulders and her eyes were fiery coals.

"What are you doing in here?" she demanded.

Frightened, Laurel burst into tears.

A lavender dusk had fallen over the garden when Leland came through the gate that evening. There were no lamps lighted yet. He set down his medical bag and stood for a few minutes, sorting through the day's mail on the hall table.

Then he lifted his head. What was that noise? It sounded like soft singing, somehow familiar. It had a low sweet melody he had not heard in a long time.

As he climbed the stairway, the music became clearer. Puzzled, he moved along the hall toward his wife's sitting room. At the door he paused. What he saw made his heart leap.

A soft violet light filtered through the filmy curtains. Through the shadows, he could see his wife seated in her rocker. There, on her lap, sat the little orphan, her head gently resting on Ava's shoulder. In one instant, he remembered the song: It was the lullaby his wife had always sung when rocking their daughter, Dorie, to sleep.

Later that night, Leland cradled his wife in his arms. She wept quietly.

"Oh, Lee, I scared her into tears!" she sobbed. "I'm so ashamed. I've been so selfish, so wrapped up in my own feelings. Can you forgive me?"

"There's nothing to forgive, my darling," he murmured, smoothing back the dark hair from her forehead. "All I've ever wanted is your happiness."

"We'll be happy again, Lee. I feel it. I know it! And I promise you this will be a home for Laurel to be happy in too."

A few weeks after her arrival, Laurel walked into Sunday school one morning. There sat her friend Kit! Within minutes, Toddy walked in too. The girls excitedly shared all their news. The Hansens, a farming family who lived near town, had adopted Kit. Toddy was living with Olivia Hale, a wealthy widow with an invalid granddaughter named Helene.

True to his word, Dr. Woodward invited the girls over to play that day, but only Toddy could come. Mrs. Hansen said Kit had too many chores. However, the girls were able to get together here and there. On the Fourth of July, they even enjoyed the colorful fireworks from the Hale house, the mansion on the hill where Toddy now lived.

The summer months quickly sped into fall. One afternoon in early September, Dr. Woodward looked in the door of Ava's sitting room. Every surface and space was covered with all sorts of fabric in every color and pattern.

"What's all this?" he asked in amazement. "A circus?"

Sitting in a pile of jumbled cloth, Laurel giggled as she always did at Dr. Woodward's jokes.

"No, silly," Ava replied, holding up a length of material. "We're choosing material for Laurel's school clothes. Mrs. Danby is coming tomorrow, and it's going to be a week of selecting patterns, cutting, fitting, and pinning. You're going to be completely surrounded by sewing women!"

"I was right," he laughed. "It will be a circus! Maybe I'd better take the week off and go fishing."

"Nothing of the kind, Lee. We need your opinion," Ava said, pretending to be stern. "You have excellent taste."

Dr. Woodward raised his eyebrows. "Mrs. Danby doesn't think so!" he declared. "The last time she was here, she glared at me every time I walked in. I think she thought I was going to perform surgery on her sewing machine."

At this, Laurel rolled over in a fit of giggles.

"At least someone appreciates me," he added, nodding toward his little one.

"I appreciate you too, Lee. Didn't I just say as much?" Ava held up a colorful swatch. "What do you think of this?"

Leland took the piece and draped it around his wife's shoulders. "Lovely. Pink is your color. I've always loved you in it," he said. "The first time I ever saw you, you were wearing pink."

"Actually, it was dusty rose, Lee, and this is coral." Ava smiled.

"Whatever it is, you looked ravishing," he gently teased as he leaned over to kiss her.

They each smiled and then held out their arms toward Laurel. The little girl scrambled over the mountain of material and into their embrace.

"I'd better get out of here and let you ladies get on with your work," Dr. Woodward said as he started toward the door.

Ava had already turned toward Laurel. "This would be a becoming color, Laurel," she said as she held up a rose material. "We can have Mrs. Danby make it into a little suit with a short jacket and lace collar."

Leland paused at the door. For a moment, he remembered his talk with Laurel just a few days earlier. He had explained about Dorie. "You see, Laurel," he had told her as they sat together on the front porch, "we lost our little girl just like you lost your parents. The three of us can help each other now. You'll be our little girl and we'll be your parents."

It gladdened the doctor's heart to see them both so happy. Ava's headaches had almost disappeared, and she was now completely absorbed in getting the child ready for school. Little Laurel was delighting in all the attention. Things were beginning to change for the better at last.

Mrs. Danby, the town's best seamstress, arrived at eight o'clock the next morning to take possession of the upstairs spare room. Laurel stood patiently while she knelt on the floor draping, tucking, and hemming. The little girl kept wondering when the dressmaker was going to swallow one of the straight pins she kept in her mouth. To Laurel's amazement, the seamstress never did!

The result was a complete new wardrobe for Laurel one week later. Besides four new school dresses, there was a Sunday-best outfit, blouses, jumpers, skirts, and jackets, as well as new camisoles, petticoats, and bloomers.

On the first morning of school, Dr. Woodward sent Jenny upstairs to see what was taking Laurel so long.

Jenny walked into the room to discover Laurel still in her petticoat, staring into the open armoire filled with her new clothes.

"My land, Laurel, you'll have all the other girls green with envy!" she remarked with her hands on her hips. "What're you planning to wear?"

Wrinkles had already formed on the little girl's brow. "I don't know."

"Didn't Mrs. Woodward tell you what to wear?"

Laurel shook her head. She had never had to pick out her clothes before. Her mama had always laid out her clothes each morning, and at Greystone, there had never been any choice.

"Well, come on then," Jenny said, a twinkle in her perky eyes. "I'll help you. You mustn't be late the first day of school."

The maid studied the contents of the armoire for a few moments then pulled out a bright blue dress trimmed with darker blue braid. "How about this?" she asked, holding it up for Laurel's approval. "Here, let me help you."

She slipped the dress over Laurel's head, guided her arms into the sleeves, and buttoned the dozen small buttons up the back. When she got to the top, the chain from Laurel's locket accidentally caught. Jenny fumbled to untangle it.

"I'd better unfasten this clasp, Laurel," she told her.

"No!" Laurel jerked away from Jenny with both hands at her neck holding the chain.

Startled, Jenny stared at her. "What's the matter—"

"I can't ever take off this chain! Not ever!" Her eyes were filling with tears.

Still puzzled, Jenny explained, "I meant just until I got the top button done."

"I can't take it off, Jenny, because Mama told me not to."

"But Mrs. Woodward would understand—"

"I don't mean her," the youngster cried. "She's not my mama!" The little girl opened the small, heart-shaped locket. "This is my real mama, and this is my real father."

The young maid studied the faces of the lovely, dark-eyed young woman and the handsome young man. Her thoughts were mixed. What would the Woodwards think if they had seen Laurel respond like that? They thought of her as their daughter now. Would Laurel ever be able to love them with the same kind of heart love?

"I'm sorry, Jenny." Laurel had calmed down. "I didn't mean to yell at you."

"All right," Jenny replied, still worried. "Now turn around and I'll button more carefully so we won't catch the chain. We have to hurry now. Dr. Lee's waitin' to drive you to school."

As she entered the fenced schoolyard of Meadowridge Grammar School, Laurel's hand tightened around the lunch bag Ella had made for her. She felt her mouth go dry when she tried to swallow. As a new student, Laurel was thankful Dr. Lee was walking in with her. The school seemed so big, and she didn't know how to find the third grade classroom all by herself.

When they reached it, a pretty young woman stood at the door. "You must be Laurel. I'm Miss Cady, your teacher this year. Why don't you come in and put your things in one of the desks?"

The doctor bent down to give Laurel a kiss and a wink. "I'll see you after school."

Laurel walked into the classroom. Some other children were already there, hanging up their coats and putting their lunch bags in their desks. Of course, Laurel didn't know any of them. However, as she was putting her lunch bag away, Kit walked in. Glad to see her, Laurel waved. Not long after this, Toddy arrived, dressed in a brand-new yellow dress with matching ribbons. The three friends settled at nearby desks, together again at last.

Going to school marked the beginning of a happy period in Laurel's life. Every morning Ella packed a delicious lunch for her, and then Dr. Woodward walked her to the gate and saw her off. Sometimes he walked with her to the corner of the street, where she waited for Toddy to come down the hill from the Hale house. Then the two girls went the rest of the way together. Kit would often be waiting for them in the schoolyard. Although they were each in different homes, their friendship was as close as it had been at Greystone.

At least twice a week, Ava met Laurel at school. Ava always had a surprise or treat for her. Sometimes it was a stop at the sweet shop for a soda or a shopping trip for new hair ribbons. Other times it was just going home hand in hand for a tea party with little frosted cakes and lemonade, or hot cocoa when the weather turned cooler.

What Laurel liked best was to curl up beside Ava in the love seat and have her read out of one of the big, beautiful books from the bookshelves in Dorie's room, to which Laurel now had access.

Laurel's favorite story was the one about the Chinese princess and her singing bird. She always cuddled close to Ava, relishing the sweet smell of her rose cologne, when in her low, soft voice, Ava began, "Once upon a time, in a faraway land called China, a little girl named Kim Li lived in a great palace. Her father the emperor gave her everything her heart desired. She had all the toys, dolls, and books a child could want. This made the little girl a bit spoiled and selfish. She had only to snap her fingers and servants brought her anything she wanted."

Laurel would nod her head and try to snap her fingers at this part. Ava would smile and continue, "One day a lovely bird flew onto the railing of her balcony and sang a beautiful trilling song. It was the prettiest bird and the sweetest melody Kim Li had ever heard. But then the bird flew away. Kim Li was very unhappy. She wanted the bird to stay and go on singing."

In response to this, Laurel would pull a sad face. Ava would turn the page and read, "The next day when the bird came back, Kim Li was overjoyed. The bird sang another lovely song and again flew away. The princess went into a tantrum. She cried, stamped her feet, and banged her fist on the railing of the balcony. She wanted the bird to come back and sing to her. In fact, she wanted the bird to be there always to sing any time she wished. So she ordered her servants to get a beautiful, golden cage. The next time the bird came to perch on the balcony railing, they caught it with a net and put it in the cage. The princess was happy. Now she had the bird forever, and she could hear its song whenever she wanted."

Laurel would straighten up, holding her breath, for she knew the story by heart and knew what would come next.

"But an unexpected thing happened. In the cage, the bird would not sing. His little head drooped, his wings went limp, and he sat at the bottom of the cage. Not a note of melody came from him. The princess was angry. She shook the cage and scolded and pouted and cried. No matter what she did, the bird refused to sing.

"Finally, a servant, an old wise man, told her that if she would let the bird go free, he would come back and sing to her once more.

"The princess was astonished at such words. 'A princess can do whatever she wants, can't she?' she demanded.

"The old man shook his head. 'Music comes only when the heart is free,' he told her. 'The bird sang to you because he loved to make you happy. It was his nature to be free and sing. When he was caged, he could not be true to his nature.'

"The little princess thought for a minute. Then she opened the door of the cage, and the little bird flew out and away. Kim Li was sad. She thought she would never see the bird again or listen to his song, but—"

Here Ava would stop. Laurel had heard the story so often she knew how it ended and would finish it.

"But the very next day the bird *did* come back and sang the sweetest song she had ever heard. Right, Mother?"

"Right, darling!" Ava would laugh and hug Laurel.

Besides reading together, they soon discovered another common interest. Ava sometimes played the piano. One day she left the lid of the keyboard open, and Laurel came into the parlor and picked out the simple tune of "Twinkle, Twinkle, Little Star" from memory. Ava, hearing her from the dining room where she was polishing silver, asked, "Where did you learn that?"

"My mama taught me."

"Then maybe we should see that you have piano lessons."

Laurel came almost to regret that impulse because Ava, determined to give Laurel every possible advantage, wasted no time. She immediately arranged for Laurel to go to Miss Millie Webb's, the church organist, for lessons twice a week. Ava also insisted that Laurel practice diligently. Laurel progressed rapidly, and Ava gloried in every new and more difficult piece Laurel mastered. As Laurel grew up, she understood that having an accomplished daughter fulfilled some deep need in Ava.

Being the center of the Woodwards' life might have spoiled Laurel. Somehow it didn't. She accepted their devotion and did her best to return their love. She was more and more aware of how lucky she was to have been placed out with them in contrast to the situations of her two best friends.

Toddy, although living in the luxurious home of Olivia Hale as companion to the invalid Helene, whose physical ups and downs the household revolved around, had to conform to a very rigid schedule. Kit's lot was even worse. She was hardly more than a hired girl at the Hansen farm. Laurel often felt guilty about all her pretty clothes when Kit wore the same patched dress year after year, hems obviously let down, sleeves lengthened.

Yes, Laurel was completely convinced she was the lucky one of the trio.

8

Christmas 1894

The Christmas program put on by the schoolchildren in the church social hall had been a great success. As parents congratulated Miss Cady on the performance, the three friends enjoyed the refreshments.

"I'm glad I got to read your poem tonight, Kit," Toddy said as she forked up a large bite of applesauce cake from her red and green plate.

"You read it so well, Toddy," Kit replied. "You made it sound better than I thought it was when I wrote it. And Laurel's solo was great. Were you nervous?"

"I sure was." Laurel took a sip of her hot cider, then added, "But 'Silent Night' is one of my favorite carols. My mama taught it to me."

"Just think, no school for ten whole days!" Toddy bounced in her chair, setting her red curls bouncing. "And if it keeps on snowing, we can go sledding."

"I don't have a sled," Laurel said.

"Well, you'll probably get one for Christmas," Toddy told her confidently. "Lots of folks put in orders for sleds to give their children for presents. Helene told me so the other night while we were reading."

"Well, maybe," Laurel started to brighten up until she realized that Kit wasn't saying anything. Laurel's heart ached for her friend; she knew there would be no such things as sleds for Christmas at the Hansen farm.

Soon people began searching for their wraps and boots as they prepared to leave.

"Promise you'll come over and see our tree," Toddy called back to her two friends as she went to join Helene and Mrs. Hale near the door. "It touches the ceiling of our parlor!"

A few moments later, Dr. Woodward helped Ava and Laurel into the buggy then wrapped a warm rug around their knees. A gently falling snow covered the rooftops of the quaint houses and lawns along the way home, muting the sound of the horse's hooves and buggy wheels.

"Tired, darling?" Ava put her arm around Laurel's shoulder and drew her close. Laurel tucked her hands in her new white fur muff and adjusted her matching tam, two early Christmas presents from the Woodwards.

"Would you like a cup of cocoa, Laurel?" Ava asked as she and her daughter walked into the house. "I'm going to make some. I got cold on our drive home."

Laurel saw her chance. "No, thank you," she replied. "I had hot cider after the program. I think I'll get ready for bed." She kissed Ava good night and went up the stairs. She could wait until the Woodwards were in the kitchen having cocoa, then she could slip downstairs and place her gifts for them under the tree.

A few minutes later, Leland walked through the back door after taking care of the horse to find his wife still standing at the bottom of the front room stairs. She had not even taken off her hat or coat.

"Oh, Leland!" Ava exclaimed. "Laurel is such a treasure. We're so blessed."

"I couldn't agree more, my dear."

Ava removed her hat and veil and placed them on the hall table while Leland helped her with her fur-collared cape.

"And she has the voice of an angel."

"She sang very nicely indeed."

"Nicely?" Ava eyed her reflection in the hall mirror and turned around with a small frown. "Is that all you have to say about it?"

"Well, I'm no music critic."

"You don't have to be to recognize talent like that." Ava grabbed her husband's arm to turn him toward the kitchen. "Come have a cup of cocoa with me. I want to tell you what I'm thinking."

Once seated at the kitchen table, Ava's voice became serious. "Leland, we must see that Laurel's voice is properly trained. Whom should I ask about a voice teacher for her? Mr. Fordyce, the music teacher at the high school?"

"I have no idea," he shook his head. "There's plenty of time."

"Not really. I've read it's important to start early. We must see that she doesn't acquire any bad habits and learns to breathe correctly."

"Laurel's only twelve, darling," Lee protested gently.

"You think I'm being silly, don't you?" Ava accused.

"No, not silly, my dear. Maybe just overestimating Laurel's talent and desire. Maybe she isn't interested in developing her voice."

"But it's up to us as her parents to guide her. We have a responsibility to see that she appreciates her gift and cultivates it." Ava's voice grew firmer. "Didn't you hear the comments tonight? Everyone was complimenting her. She has a gift, Leland, and I intend to see that she doesn't waste it."

Unknown to either of them, Laurel, standing in the hall with the Christmas gifts in her arms, had overheard their conversation.

A treasured memory quietly surfaced in her mind. She remembered sitting at the piano while Mama played and together they sang all the lovely old songs. "Why, Laurel, you sound just like a little lark!" her mama would say.

Christmas had always been a special time for the two of them. Even though they had only a tiny tree set on the table and a few little gifts, it was special because Mama made it so. Laurel closed her eyes. She could almost see it again, the candles, the piano, Mama's beautiful smile.

Whenever she sang, she sang for her mama.

The Class of 1900

"All ready for the senior picnic?"

Laurel stood at the hall mirror retying the bow at the collar of her pink shirtwaist.

"Yes, Papa Lee." Laurel whirled around to greet him. "I'm waiting for Dan. He'll be here in a few minutes. We're going to walk over to school and meet the class, then take hay wagons out to Riverview Park."

"That sounds like fun." He smiled. "Well, I have office hours this morning, so I'd better get going. Have a good time."

"We will, Papa. Thanks." Laurel offered her soft cheek for a kiss.

Leland went out the side door and stopped in the garden to pick a rosebud to put in the lapel of his jacket. At fifty, the doctor was still handsome, with strong features and a pleasant smile. There was more silver in his thick wavy hair now, but with his lean build he had the appearance of a much younger man.

A short while later he stood at the window of his office at the back of the house, watching Laurel and Dan

Brooks go out the front gate together. His eyes followed his daughter's graceful figure as she walked beside her tall friend from Meadowridge High. Laurel had turned into a beautiful young lady. Dan was a likeable fellow, courteous, intelligent, and dependable. If Leland had had a son of his own, he would have wanted one like Dan.

The doctor sighed. Was it possible it had been ten years since the little seven-year-old girl had come into their home?

"Lee, still alone? No patients yet?"

Ava's voice interrupted his thoughts, and Leland turned to see her face peering around the office door.

"Yes, I mean, no—I'm alone, no patients. Come in," he invited.

Ava slipped in and closed the door quietly behind her.

Looking at her, Leland was struck as he always was. She seemed to grow lovelier with each passing year. Her figure was still girlishly slim, the dark hair still untouched by a single strand of gray, her skin pale and smooth. At the moment, however, a small anxious frown cast two vertical lines between Ava's dark, winged brows. Her expression alerted him that something was troubling her.

"What is it, Ava? What's wrong?"

As he took both of her hands in his, he discovered they were icy.

"I'm worried, Lee," she began, "about Dan."

"Dan?" The doctor repeated.

"Yes. He's taken Laurel to every single graduation event. I'm afraid he's going to be disappointed." Ava sat down in the straight-backed chair next to her husband's desk, her filmy white dress flowing to the floor.

"Disappointed about what?" Leland stepped back and propped himself against his desk.

"You and I both know about what," she replied. "Laurel. Dan's totally unsuitable for Laurel, and he's going to be disappointed."

Leland started to laugh. "Ava, let's not borrow trouble. Dan's applied to medical school. He's got long years of study ahead. He hasn't time to be serious about anything but his education."

"Well—"

An internal alarm sounded in Leland's mind. It worried the doctor that his wife was so possessive of their daughter. Laurel was nearly eighteen now, almost grown up. Soon they would both have to face the fact that someday she would leave. He hoped Ava would be able to handle it.

The doctor didn't let his thoughts go any further. "Why don't you find something else to do, my dear? Those two youngsters are going out to have a wonderful day on a picnic."

After the picnic, most of the seniors paired off and left the area to roam along the wooded paths through the park or follow the trail down to the river.

Dan and Laurel climbed up the hillside to the meadow overlooking the river and settled under the shade of a gnarled, old oak tree. The afternoon seemed to stretch endlessly under a lazy sky. The hum of insects among the wildflowers in the tall grass floated on sweet-scented summer air. The air was warm and drowsy.

Laurel leaned her head back against the tree, feeling the roughness of its bark through the thin material of her blouse. With eyes half closed, she could see Dan. His head was turned so that his profile was outlined against the cloudless blue sky. They had been friends now since elementary school. Aside from Kit and Toddy, Dan was probably the closest friend she had in Meadowridge. As her mind drifted, she began silently to rehearse the lyrics of the songs she would be singing at the upcoming honors banquet.

All of a sudden, Dan raised himself to a sitting position, reached for her hand, and kissed the tips of her fingers. Laurel met his earnest brown eyes.

"Laurel, we've known each other since elementary school." The young man paused then said, "I love you."

"Oh, Dan, I wish you wouldn't say that," she protested. "I care about you, you know that, but we're both . . . well, we're just getting out of high school. We have our whole lives ahead of us."

"Don't you ever daydream about the future, Laurel?"

"Of course I do," she replied, stopping short. Certainly, she daydreamed about the future, but she never shared her dreams with anyone. They were her secret, and she planned to keep them that way.

Laurel watched Dan get to his feet, pick up some small stones, and skim them across the wide river. Yes, she dreamed. She dreamed about the man she would marry one day, how they would meet. What would he look like? Laurel hoped he would be handsome and kind and would love the things she loved, like music and reading.

She fingered her locket. Yes, she dreamed. About her past, her parents, who she really was. Where had they come from? Was her grandmother alive? What had her mama meant about meeting her grandmother when all was forgiven?

One day Laurel hoped to return to Boston. She would find the old apartment house and ring the doorbell and Mrs. Campbell would come to the door. The cheerful landlady would take her to the top floor and unlock the door. Everything in their apartment would be just the same as the last time she had seen it.

Laurel would go through it, room by room. She would find the upright piano with the candleholders on either side of the music rack. Her father's painting of the lighthouse would still hang over the piano, her mother's rocker near the window. In the bedroom, Laurel could picture the trundle bed they pulled out from under Mama's high poster bed. And her beloved Miranda would still be sleeping peacefully on top of its covers.

It was not that Laurel was unhappy. Her life with the Woodwards was nearly perfect. Papa Lee and Mother were a loving, caring couple. But all through the years, Laurel had clung to the memories of her life before Meadowridge like a drowning person clutching at a straw. If she let them go, they would drift down the stream and be swept into the rushing current. She couldn't take that chance. Her memories were too special, too important to her life. If she lost them, she might lose her mama, and she could never do that.

"Come on, Laurel. Everyone's starting back."

Dan's voice broke into her thoughts. She opened her eyes, blinking into the bright sunshine. He held his hand out and pulled her to her feet.

As they walked back down the hill to the wagons, Dan took Laurel's hand.

"About the class dance, Laurel—" he began.

"I told you I'd have to see, Dan," she reminded him gently. "If Mother and Papa Lee say it's all right, I'll go with you. But you know how easily Mother's feelings get hurt."

Dan decided not to argue. Pressuring her would only make things more difficult. He'd just have to wait and see.

10

On the afternoon of the honors banquet, Laurel walked over to the high school to rehearse the songs she was singing that night.

This last week of the school year, the building was nearly empty. A few students were sitting in the sunshine looking at the yearbook when Laurel went up the steps and inside. As she walked down the deserted corridor, she heard the sound of a trumpet solo. She opened the door to the music room and quietly took a seat at the back. The boy with the trumpet struggled until Mr. Fordyce finally spoke to him.

"That's enough for today, Billy. You need some practice, young fellow. Guess we've had too much baseball weather lately, eh?" He tousled the youngster's hair.

"Yes, sir," the boy mumbled, getting to his feet.

As the student scuffled about packing up his instrument, the teacher spotted Laurel.

"All right, Laurel, it's time for us now. Let's begin with scales before we go into your numbers."

Laurel adjusted the music stand and placed her music sheets on it. When Mr. Fordyce struck the first note, she took a deep breath and began. Less than an hour later, he stopped playing.

"There, that's it. I think we're through for today. You can overrehearse, you know."

Laurel was surprised. Usually, her music teacher made her go through pieces over and over. This time he was standing up, gathering his music, and about to shut the lid over the keyboard.

"Then it sounded all right?"

"It was fine, Laurel. You'll do splendidly, I'm sure."

Something wasn't right. Laurel stood uncertainly, wondering what was wrong. Finally, she asked, "Mr. Fordyce, did I do something wrong?"

"No, not at all, Laurel. Everything was fine, on pitch. Be sure to rest your voice for the next few hours though. Drink some hot lemonade before the performance."

Laurel wasn't satisfied. "Is that all?"

The teacher continued busily stacking music sheets. Then he turned toward her. "I guess I've been wondering what your plans are after graduation."

"I'm not sure," she replied.

Mr. Fordyce opened his briefcase to stuff the music sheets inside. When he looked up again, his expression was serious. "No plans? What about your voice?"

"I want to continue my lessons through the summer, that is if—"

"Laurel, I'm not talking about this summer." He snapped the case shut. "You have a voice. Don't you care about it? Dozens of others would die for what you have." He sighed heavily. "Laurel, I've taught you all I can. I can't do any more to help you develop your talent."

Laurel stared at him.

"Laurel, you have to *know* this. I can't tell you. You have to *want* it for yourself. Some things can't be taught. For a singer, there has to be that something on the inside that tells her she'll die if she can't learn everything there is to know about singing." He shook his head. "If you don't feel this, Laurel, well, I don't know what else to say."

"But where would I go? Who could I find to teach me?"

"You'd have to go somewhere like Chicago or Boston where there's a music conservatory. There are teachers there who can give you what you need." He paused. "Haven't you even discussed the possibility with your parents? I'm sure they could afford to send you."

"No," Laurel replied as she picked up her music. "I guess we just assumed I'd keep on taking lessons from you and singing in the choir."

Mr. Fordyce looked amazed. "Forgive me, Laurel, but it would be a tragedy to waste such talent as yours. You should sit down with your parents and discuss this seriously. In fact, if you like, I'll talk to them, maybe suggest a school for you."

Laurel felt suddenly confused. "I don't know, Mr. Fordyce. I'll have to think about it."

Outside, Laurel headed for Meadowridge Park. She couldn't go home right now. She found a bench near the duck pond and sat down.

Her mind would not stop racing and she felt shaky but excited. Although she tried to remember everything Mr. Fordyce had said, she had really heard only one word: *Boston!* If Laurel could go to Boston, she could trace her real parents' background and find out about her mama. The hope she had carried for so long, hidden deep in her heart, burst into new life. Maybe this was the way!

Laurel had sung all her life but had never once considered her singing as something to be developed and polished, like a rare instrument. It was Mother who had insisted on her having lessons with Mr. Fordyce. Now the music teacher was suggesting something entirely different. He was talking about studying voice seriously and devoting her life to singing.

Was she ready to do this? Something strange and wonderful always happened inside her whenever she sang. She felt a lifting, soaring sensation that carried her far beyond the room or the people. It was a feeling she never experienced in any other way. Was this what Mr. Fordyce was talking about?

Three large white ducks waddled into the sparkling water. As she watched, Laurel realized that now was the time of decision. Would it be wrong to use her voice as the means to pursue her real desire? If the Woodwards would finance her musical education in Boston, she could begin to investigate the mystery of her heritage, her past. Her dream would come true.

Unconsciously, Laurel fingered the heart-shaped locket she still wore around her neck. But what about Mother? She was so protective. How would she react? Would she let Laurel go? It was too much to think about now. Laurel had the banquet tonight, then graduation and the dance. She wouldn't tell anyone just yet, not even Toddy and Kit. The whole summer lay ahead of them. She would wait.

11

The evening of graduation day, Dan walked over from Elm Street to the Woodwards' house. Dr. Woodward had agreed to let him escort Laurel to their class dance. He carried with him a small corsage of sweetheart roses.

Before ringing the doorbell, the young man adjusted his tie. Then he ran a nervous finger around the inside of his high, stiff shirt collar and straightened his new navy blue jacket.

"Good evening, Dan," Mrs. Woodward greeted him cooly. "How nice you look. Do come in."

As Ava led the way across the parlor toward the side porch, her reservations about him surfaced again. Why couldn't Leland understand that this boy was simply not suitable for their daughter? His grandmother had raised him in a house over on Elm Street of all places. All of the houses there were shabby. His mother worked as a milliner in a big city department store somewhere and hadn't been to visit him in years. No, this was not a good match at all.

Ava pushed back the glass doors to the side porch. "We'll sit here a bit. Laurel isn't quite ready," she said as she invited him to sit on one of their white wicker chairs. "She should be down soon."

Ava occupied herself by pouring them each a glass of iced tea. "What are your plans now that you've graduated, Dan?" She tried to be sociable.

"Well, I'll be working full-time for Mr. Groves at the pharmacy for the summer. In the fall, I'll be going to college."

"Oh, and where will that be?"

"I'll be going back to Ohio—"

"Ohio? Why is that?"

"Well, it's near my father's folks and—"

"Your father?" Ava was surprised.

"Yes," Dan gulped the iced tea Mrs. Woodward had just handed him. "I'll be attending State College. I can spend weekends with them, you see. They have a farm—"

A farm! No, this would never do. Ava's daughter was not going to marry someone with that kind of mixed-up background. And that was that!

Just then, the screen door opened and Dr. Woodward came out onto the porch. "Well, here I am, my dear. Hello, Dan."

Dan got to his feet as the doctor extended his hand.

Ava did not notice. Her mind was elsewhere. No, this match must be prevented before it got started, and that was all there was to it.

Meanwhile, Laurel was upstairs sliding a silver comb into a swirl of her dark hair. She stepped back from the mirror to judge the effect.

"How does this look, Jenny?" she asked.

Standing alongside, the maid nodded. "Lovely! My, how growed up you look, with your hair up and all."

"I'm supposed to look grown up, Jenny! I'm seventeen and finishing school." Laurel's laugh was high and sweet.

"Seems like just yesterday we were gettin' you dressed for your first day of elementary school." Jenny shook her head in disbelief. "Well, let's get your dress on now. Dan's here, you know."

"Yes," Laurel replied as she slipped her arms into the delicate blue-violet dress the maid was holding.

"You do look like a picture!" Jenny exclaimed as the silk material fell in ruffles over the underskirt. As Laurel eyed herself in the mirror, Jenny picked up the necklace of seed pearls from the top of the dressing table. "You're wearing this, aren't you?"

Laurel hesitated a second, her fingers secretly clutching the locket she still wore around her neck.

"I suppose Mother will wonder if I don't," she sighed. "I certainly don't want to hurt her feelings." Tucking the precious jewelry under her dress so it wouldn't be visible, she turned so Jenny could clasp the necklace around her neck.

"Thanks, Jenny," Laurel remarked as she picked up her small beaded purse and gloves.

Laurel gave her a hug, then waved and went along the hall and down the stairway.

That night, the time sped by. Not wanting to dance with anyone else, Dan was forced to stand on the sidelines watching Laurel, whose dance card had filled up very quickly.

"Ladies and gentlemen, the next dance is a Paul Jones. Ladies, make a circle, and gentlemen, form a circle around them. Everyone moves counterclockwise to the music. When it stops, whoever stands opposite from you is your partner."

"Come on, let's get into the circle!" Toddy cried, grabbing both Laurel's and Kit's hands.

The music started and the two circles began to move. Laurel quickly realized that some of the guys were trying to guess when the band was going to stop so they would wind up opposite their favorite partner. Dan was one of these. He was keeping his eye on her.

However, when the music finally stopped, Dan was standing right in front of Kit. Dressed in a simple lace-trimmed blouse and flared white skirt, Kit shone. White roses were tucked into the braided coil of her hair. She seemed happier than Laurel had ever seen her. And why not? She had been awarded a scholarship to Merrivale Teachers College.

But no, there was something else. Laurel eyed her friend carefully. Then she saw it. As Kit held out her hand to Dan, her beautiful gray eyes lit up and a sweet smile trembled on her mouth. In one brief moment, Laurel saw the truth: Kit was in love with Dan.

12

The summer was over. The maple trees along the streets of Meadowridge began turning gold, and the Virginia creeper clinging to the sides of the house blushed crimson. In the mornings, thin frost glistened on the lawns as the mist rose into the sky, blurring the sharpness of the blue line of hills surrounding the town.

Like leaves scattering in the wind, everyone would soon be going away. Toddy was leaving with Mrs. Hale and Helene to tour Europe. Dan had already left for college, and Kit would soon begin her first year at Merrivale. Only Laurel was left behind.

Returning home one September afternoon, Laurel paused to listen to a distant train whistle at the Meadowridge crossing. She sighed, unlatched the gate, and walked up the path and into the house. She had to talk to the Woodwards. She couldn't put it off any longer. She had carefully rehearsed all the reasons they ought to permit her to go. It was now or never.

She walked around to Dr. Lee's L-shaped office at the back of the house.

"Dismiss it from your mind," the doctor immediately replied when she brought up the subject. "A young lady your age traveling across the country by herself? It's out of the question."

Laurel wasn't prepared for this abrupt refusal, at least not from him.

In a voice that shook, she pleaded, "Will you at least think about it, Papa Lee? Discuss it with Mother?"

"Discuss what with me?" a voice behind her asked. Laurel turned to see Ava standing in the office doorway, her arms filled with purple asters from the flower garden.

The scene that followed was worse than Laurel could have imagined. Ava's face turned pale as she laid the bouquet of flowers on a nearby table.

"But you can't possibly go so far. And alone! No, I won't hear of it." Ava's eyes looked dark and fearful. "Leland, talk to her!"

Laurel looked helplessly at Dr. Woodward. The handsome face that had always regarded her with such indulgent love was now grave. The eyes that always looked at her with affectionate warmth seemed cool.

Laurel turned toward Ava, who stood like a statue in the middle of the room. "But, Mother, you were the one who wanted me to study voice in the first place. It was you who said I have a gift. I'd never have taken lessons if you hadn't encouraged me."

"But I never dreamed it would take you away from us. Of course you have a gift, Laurel, and I want you to go on with your lessons."

Laurel pressed on. "Mr. Fordyce says he's taught me all he can. He says I need further training elsewhere, at a music conservatory."

"To do what?" Ava flung out her hands in a helpless gesture. "To become a professional singer? To go on the stage? I never heard of such nonsense." She turned toward Leland. "What is Milton Fordyce thinking of to put such ideas into a young girl's head?"

"Papa—"

The doctor held up his hand in a warning. "I don't think we should discuss this any further right now. I have patients coming in a few minutes, and we all need to calm down." He looked at his wife. "Ava, my dear, there's no use upsetting yourself. Nothing will be settled right away. We can talk about this later, when we're all more composed."

But they didn't. Laurel waited and waited, but no one said anything. Everything went on as before and yet everything had changed. Ava seemed anxious, and her face had a pinched look. Her every glance expressed reproach at Laurel's wanting to leave them.

Dr. Lee always found an excuse to be with a patient or have paperwork to do. He was having a hard time facing this even though he had known his little girl was growing up. The doctor placed his pen down on the pile of papers at his desk. He couldn't work right now. His mind wouldn't cooperate.

Torn between his love for the two women in his life, Leland didn't know what to do. Ava's life revolved around Laurel. She was attending church and had become involved with people again. Her headaches had almost disappeared. What would this sudden change do to her emotional health? Leland couldn't bear the thought that his wife might plunge back into the darkness of depression.

The doctor leaned back in his desk chair. His life, too, centered on Laurel. To lose another daughter! The very thought sent a stabbing pain through his heart. He realized Laurel was a young woman now. Launching her into adulthood had been part of the plan. Yet how had it happened so fast? Where had the years gone?

Leland sighed. He knew Laurel well enough to know she had already made up her mind. As her father, he yearned to help her, but he didn't know if he could face this. The deep wounds of a loss he had once known had somehow begun to hurt again.

Ava had begun to spend more time in Dorie's old room sitting on the floor by the window seat. Getting upset always brought on one of her headaches, and now they were coming back. It had taken so long to work through the grief of losing Dorie.

Laurel was struggling with her conscience. On the one hand, she wanted to please the Woodwards. They had been so good to her all these years, and she loved them dearly. She did not want to hurt them. But if they didn't believe in her talent, why had they encouraged her? Laurel knew she was changing. Something new was beginning to happen on the inside. It was both disturbing and appealing. Was it wrong to want to leave? What would happen to her if she did? Laurel found herself torn between loyalty to her secret dream and her love for the Woodwards.

That Christmas, Laurel rehearsed with the choir for the annual performance of the *Messiah*. Everyone hailed it as the finest program Meadowridge Community

Church choir had ever presented. Afterward the church held a reception in the decorated social hall. It was the custom to hang small cornucopias on the church Christmas tree. Inside each was a slip of paper bearing a Scripture verse, each person's special Bible message for the coming year.

Laurel opened hers. It read: "Be strong and of a good courage; be not afraid, neither be thou dismayed: for the LORD thy God is with thee whithersoever thou goest" (Josh. 1:9). Laurel read the words again. Somehow they struck a chord in her heart, the right note. God would be with her! Laurel realized she had been battling fear. This Scripture passage was telling her to be strong and not afraid. It was confirmation. She *must* go to Boston.

The week after New Year's, Laurel gathered up her courage to talk to Dr. Lee. The sun was streaming through his office windows. A roaring fire in the Franklin stove took the chill off the January morning. The smell of old leather from the shelves of medical books mixed with the spicy pine scent of the burning wood.

Dr. Woodward looked up from his desk. His kind blue eyes met hers. Laurel noticed that his thick gray hair was beginning to turn silver.

"Papa Lee," Laurel's words came slowly, "I've written the music conservatory in Boston for an application."

The swivel chair on which the doctor sat creaked. Then, the only sound was the crackling wood in the stove. Leland didn't move. He couldn't move.

Finally, he asked, "Do you have any idea what this will do to your mother?"

The last thing she wanted to do was to hurt these two wonderful people, but she knew what she had to do. This was her destiny. She had to be true to herself, whatever the cost, whether they understood it or not.

"Papa Lee, I have to go," she begged. "Please don't make it any harder than it already is."

Leland looked out at the trees, bare and without color. He felt the same. With Laurel gone, all the color in his life would be gone too. Could he live through it again? Could he lose another daughter? Suddenly, he felt old, very old.

"When will you go, Laurel?" His words were quiet, almost without life.

Laurel's heart thumped inside her chest. This was harder than she imagined. Everything within her wanted to run and jump in his lap, like the old days. The little girl inside yearned to swing on the porch and laugh again. Why did this have to be so hard?

But no, she had to remain strong. This was too important. "Within the week," she replied.

The next week at the Woodward house was the most difficult Laurel had ever known. At night, when she heard Ava's muffled sobs, she wanted to run into her room and comfort her. But Laurel knew the only way to do that would be not to go at all, and she couldn't do that.

The morning of her departure came at last. A gray, wet mist cloaked the barren trees outside her bedroom window. Her train departed at seven. Laurel dressed and carried her suitcase downstairs. She stood in the front hall, straining to hear some movement upstairs. There was none.

As she stood at the hall mirror putting on her hat, she spotted an envelope propped against the vase. In Dr. Woodward's bold scribble was her name. The young woman picked it up and opened it. Inside were five crisp twenty-dollar bills and two fifty-dollar bills. But there was no note.

A moment later she caught Ella's reflection in the mirror. The sad-eyed cook stood in the archway of the dining room, sniffing and wiping her eyes with a balled-up handkerchief. Laurel felt a rush of affection for Ella, who had become her friend. The plump woman opened her arms, and Laurel walked over to hug her.

"Don't cry, Ella. I'll be back," she whispered.

"Your cab's out front," the cook managed to say as she smoothed down her wrinkled apron. "We're going to miss you, Laurel."

Laurel walked over to the foot of the stairway and stood there for a minute, looking up. Should she go back upstairs and knock at her parents' door? She wanted so badly to tell them how much she loved them, how much she would miss them both. She longed for them to understand and extend their blessing. But it wasn't meant to be.

With a sigh she put on her green wool coat and straightened the brim of her hat. She blew Ella a kiss then picked up her bags and went out into the mist-veiled morning. The door clicked loudly behind her. She was leaving this world behind, entering a new one.

The train station's platform was deserted. Except for the clerk in the office, no one was around. The wait seemed to last forever. Finally, the familiar shrill whistle and hissing steam reached her ears. The train was almost there. It rounded the bend and slowed to a stop.

"All aboard, miss." The conductor offered his hand to assist her up the high steps into the car.

Laurel remembered the first time she had stepped off onto this same platform. She had been a little lost orphan then, longing for a place to call home. She had felt alone and frightened.

She entered the nearly empty car, placed her suit-case in the rack above an empty seat, and plunked down on the scratchy red upholstery. She was taking off her hat when she heard the clug of the engine and felt the train lurch forward. As Laurel pressed her face against the window, the memory of a little seven-year-old girl looking at her reflected face as a train sped across the prairie flashed through her mind. Similar feelings of longing trickled up. She looked out the window, back toward Meadowridge. It was difficult to leave without the Woodwards' blessing.

What would happen to her now? She was alone, once again.

Boston

Boston! She was here at last! Laurel peered out the window of the hired hack. Here she was in the heart of the historical city called the "Cradle of Liberty." As she looked to the right and then to the left, she was filled with excitement. The city was alive with people and activities, a long distance from the sleepy, small-town atmosphere of Meadowridge. It bustled with noise and movement.

Laurel could not remember much about Boston from the days she had lived here with her mother as a little girl. Her memories of that time were centered on her life with Mama in the tiny upstairs flat of Mrs. Campbell's boardinghouse.

The streets were winding and rather narrow, lined with tall brick buildings. The heart of the city was a jumble of banks, businesses, and churches. Trolleys sped right down the middle of the street, fighting for space with elegant buggies and wagons loaded with produce. And right in the center was a huge park where people strolled and children played.

Laurel gave the cab driver the address of a rooming house run by a distant relative of her music teacher. "Mrs. Sombey rents only to women," Mr. Fordyce had told her before she left Meadowridge. "It'll be clean and comfortable and safe. And it's near the conservatory." Mrs. Sombey had a second-floor room available, and Laurel quickly settled in.

Laurel's heart sounded like a drum as she stood looking up at the music conservatory building. Did she really think she could be a candidate for admission at such a well-known institution as this? Well, she had come this far and she was not going to turn back now. Determined, Laurel started up the stone steps and opened the door into the lobby.

All kinds of sounds greeted her. Music floated through the doorways of a dozen practice rooms, merging into an unplanned symphony. Woodwinds, violins, cellos, pianos, and French horns blended into a kind of harmony. From somewhere she heard a soprano singing scales while a group of male and female voices sang an *a cappella* chorus.

Laurel timidly followed a sign with an arrow directing her to the administration office. In a burst of laughter, a group of chattering young people, carrying notebooks and music sheets, rushed down the main stairway. Laurel moved against the wall to let them by. A thrill of nervous excitement rippled through her. She was actually here.

An hour later, however, her anticipation had drained away. In her hand, she held a sheaf of forms to be completed before she could even apply for her first interview for admission. Laurel told herself she was just tired from the long train trip and that things would look brighter once she had gotten some rest. Unfortunately, on a rainy day a week later when she went to the conservatory, Laurel was shocked to discover she would have to audition before she could be admitted. All students had to appear before a board of the faculty. These people would listen to Laurel sing and decide whether she should be admitted. The waiting list for an audition was very long.

Laurel's heart sank. Mr. Fordyce had often told his students that a career in music was one of the most difficult professions. She had never imagined it would be so hard. Is this what she truly wanted? Doubt surfaced again. Did she have the kind of resolve he had been talking about that day during her lesson? Did she want this more than life itself?

"I know just how you feel," a young woman checking the bulletin board beside her said. "If you have a coach, your chances are better."

"A coach?" The umbrella Laurel carried felt heavier and heavier as she walked through the building. Her feet were tired too.

"Yes, some of the teachers here teach students on the side." The girl shifted her notebook, crammed full of music sheets, to the other arm. "That way, you'll be at peak when you do get an audition."

"But I don't know anyone." Laurel felt more disheartened than ever. "How do you find a coach?"

"Well, I was lucky. My violin teacher was already a recognized coach at the school," the other girl said. "Do you live here in Boston?"

"I just came. I've only been here a short time."

"You mean you don't know anyone who can help you?" The girl frowned. "Then I'd advise you to check at the office. They should have a list of teachers willing to coach." Before picking up her leather violin case, she added, "It's expensive though. They charge by the hour, and they want their money first. But it's worth it. At least, I hope it's worth it."

After the girl had left, Laurel stared at the long list of names and audition dates. She felt discouraged, but she wasn't ready to give up yet.

Somewhat downhearted, she walked through the huge front hall and pushed open the outside door. It was still raining. Buttoning the top of her coat and shifting her music notebook under one arm, she opened her umbrella to start down the steps. The next thing she knew, she had bumped right into someone!

"Oh! Sorry!" a deep male voice exclaimed.

A tall young man in a black cape lowered his umbrella to tip his hat.

Suddenly, a brisk wind whipped the hat out of his hand and sent it whirling down the steps, depositing it in a muddy puddle at the bottom of the steps.

"Oh, my!" cried Laurel in dismay.

The man only laughed. "No problem," he called back over his shoulder as he rushed down to get it.

Laurel scurried after him. By the time she reached the bottom, he was shaking the water from the brim.

"I'm dreadfully sorry. I wasn't looking where I was going," she apologized. "Is it ruined?"

"No harm done," he assured her with a big smile. "It'll dry out." As he replaced the hat on his head, he grinned. "Beastly day, isn't it?"

The man's eyes were dark and sparkled with laughter.

"Well, I must be off or I'll be late!" he said, bounding up the steps and into the building. Laurel stood there a minute longer, staring after him in spite of the chilly rain. Somehow his laugh had reminded her of Toddy, who saw humor in most situations. How she missed her old friends! Both Toddy and Kit had always been there for her when things went wrong. It seemed like everything was going wrong for her right now.

What was she going to do?

14

Within a few days of her arrival, Laurel set out on the adventure she had been waiting for. Having memorized the address when she was a little girl, Laurel hired a horse and buggy to take her back to Mrs. Campbell's house. As the gig jolted over the cobblestone street, Laurel remembered the last trip she had taken with her mama. Like today, it had been cold that day. As she relived the feelings, she pulled her warm winter coat tighter around her shoulders.

Before long, they turned onto a street that felt strangely familiar.

"Whoa!" the driver announced as he opened the flap. "This is your stop, miss."

"This is 41 Oak Drive?"

"Yep."

The street had changed completely. Gone was the entire row of old frame houses, including Mrs. Campbell's apartment house. A warehouse had been erected in its place.

"You aren't looking for one of them old row houses, are you, miss?" The driver's weathered face showed his concern.

"Yes, sir," Laurel stammered. She locked her chilly fingers together inside her fur muff.

"Why, it was destroyed years ago in a big fire. Weren't nothin' left neither. Don't think anyone was hurt though."

In one instant, all of Laurel's dreams crumbled. Everything was gone. Her hopes had suddenly been smashed on the rocks of reality.

Laurel felt more determined than ever to find some evidence of her mother's family. This meant countless, time-consuming hours of research. During the next few weeks, she spent time in the musty archives of the county records office, where she poured over old records. Most of them led her nowhere. Finally, one afternoon in February she found her parents' marriage license. Lillian Maynard and Paul Vestal! Shortly after this, she happened on the record of her father's death. Laurel combed the cemeteries in Boston looking for his grave, but she never found it. She also made the rounds of galleries and art dealers' shops, hoping she might find one of his paintings. She never found any of them either.

Then, at long last, Laurel Elaine Vestal took the hardest trip of all, to Greystone Orphanage. The trolley let her off at the bottom of a long, steep hill. Her heart was pounding as memories of that day so long ago flooded her mind. The dark, rainy Boston morning. Clutching her mother's hand. Her blue velour coat with the scalloped cape blowing in the wind. The cold stone building.

And there it stood, like a fortress, the chain-link fence surrounding it like a prison. Memories of her drab uniform, the plain food, and the third-floor dormitory flooded her mind. Thoughts of that day in Miss Clinock's office where she was told about her mother's death weakened her resolve. Could she go in? Laurel stood in front of the massive door that had latched behind her that wretched day. Everything inside her screamed no! Laurel whirled around and ran back down the hill as fast as she could. She knew right then that she couldn't go back inside that place. Not ever!

After a few weeks, Laurel's name finally appeared on the list of applicants at the conservatory, but her audition date would not be scheduled for weeks. March blew into Boston, bringing wind and cold rain and sometimes ice.

One particular morning, a sharp wind off the river cut across the common just as Laurel made her way back from the conservatory. She had gone to check the auditions list again, in case there had been a change, a cancellation perhaps. As she slanted her umbrella up against the stinging rain, she wondered why she hadn't heard from Mr. Fordyce yet. She had written him, asking for his help with the three recommendations she was required to have.

As she hurried along, the day seemed particularly dreary. She was having a hard time not feeling depressed. She had never dreamed living on her own in a city would be so expensive. Everything cost so much more here. The money Dr. Woodward had given her was almost gone. She would have to find work soon, but what kind? What could she do to earn something to stretch her small amount of cash? Silently, she prayed for an idea.

Since she didn't really want to return to her small room at the boardinghouse, Laurel decided to go to the small Italian restaurant on the corner. Pushing open the door, she immediately felt its warmth and smelled the delicious fragrance of freshly baked bread and newly brewed coffee.

After giving the waitress her order, she gazed out the front picture window from her small table in the corner. Homesickness filled her young heart. She missed Meadowridge and her room. She missed Toddy and Kit and even Dan. She especially missed Papa Lee and Mother.

"Here we are, miss," the blond-haired waitress announced cheerily.

A bowl of chunky vegetable soup with a buttery slice of crusty, warm homemade bread revived Laurel's spirits. She was sipping one of the last spoonfuls of soup when a thought popped into her head. A piano teacher! She instantly liked the idea. Why not? She knew how to play the piano, and she could teach children. This would enable her to bring in some extra money while she was waiting for her audition. She decided to give it a try. She would place an advertisement in the Boston newspaper right away.

"Is everything all right, miss?" the waitress interrupted her thoughts.

"Yes, thank you. It was delicious," she said, dabbing her mouth with the checkered linen napkin. She looked out the restaurant window into the rain-swept street. Wet brown leaves cluttered the edge. The sound of jingling harnesses reached her ears as a horse and buggy trotted by. In spite of the chilly misting rain, Laurel spotted a few pedestrians scurrying along the sidewalk toward unknown destinations.

All at once, the memory of her mother came to mind. Lillian Vestal had been forced to work as a music teacher here in Boston to support herself and her small child. This was exactly what Laurel was about to do! How lonely her mother must have felt trying to raise a child in this big city all by herself. How lonely Laurel was beginning to feel now with no one she knew anywhere close by.

She fingered her heart-shaped locket, trying to bring her mama's face into clear focus in her mind. Instead, it was two other faces she saw: Ava and Dr. Lee. The memory struck her conscience. Ava looked drawn and white, with purple shadows under her eyes. And Dr. Lee. How sad he looked the last time he told her good night. She missed them both. She could hardly bear to think of it. She knew she had broken their hearts, but her own heart was breaking too.

"Will there be anything else?" The waitress pulled her writing pad out of the pocket of her striped apron. "For dessert today, we've got caramel custard, and Maria just pulled an apple cobbler out of the oven."

Laurel's mouth watered at the suggestions, but she shook her head. Until she had a job, she had to watch her pennies.

At that moment, the restaurant door burst open. With a gust of wind and rain, a young man dashed inside. As he closed his wet umbrella, he shook it and showered a few customers nearby.

"Sorry," he said in a deep voice. "I do beg your pardon."

Laurel recognized that voice. It was the same young man she had met on the steps of the conservatory a few weeks ago.

Mr. Pasquini, the restaurant owner, hurried forward. "Welcome, welcome! How was the tour?"

"*Bravissimo!*" He replied as he took off his overcoat. "Better than we expected. Sold-out crowds every night." He hung his dripping coat on the wooden cloak tree near the door. "But I missed your wonderful pasta, and no one can make bread like Maria."

"Well, come along. Sit, sit!" The owner's round face beamed as he ushered him to a seat. "First some minestrone, yes? Then maybe some linguini?"

The newcomer rubbed his hands together in anticipation. "Fine," he smiled as he sat down.

Laurel couldn't help noticing how handsome this young man was. His dark complexion made her think he might be Italian. He was certainly at home here. As she glanced his way, he met her gaze. She quickly looked down at her empty soup bowl. For some reason her heart jumped unexpectedly.

Having finished lunch, she gathered her coat and went up to the cash register to pay. Mr. Pasquini hovered at the table of the young man in lively conversation. Laurel got her change and walked out the door into the stormy March day.

Her decision to advertise for piano pupils now settled, she decided to look for a newspaper. She headed for a corner newsstand about a block from where she lived. By the time she reached the newsstand, the hem of her coat and dress were soaked, and she could feel the damp seeping in through her thin leather shoes.

Miserable and shivering, she hurried along the slick sidewalk. Chilled to the bone, she finally reached the boardinghouse and mounted the narrow stairway to her second-floor room. She longed for Ella's cozy kitchen where she would find hot chocolate or spice tea and homemade cookies on a day like this.

Laurel quickly removed her wet clothes and curled up at the end of the bed. As she spread the damp newspaper out in front of her to turn to the classified section, an item on the social page caught her eye.

"Mrs. Bennett Maynard will host an evening party next Tuesday evening to benefit the Boston Symphony."

The name leaped at Laurel from the wet page. *Mrs. Bennett Maynard!* Her mother's maiden name had been Maynard. Could this woman be the grandmother Laurel never knew? Her heart almost skipped a beat. The article listed her address in the most exclusive residential section of town, Wembley Square.

She would have to go there.

The next morning, Laurel awakened with a nasty sore throat. For the next two weeks, she lay in bed with laryngitis and a heavy cold, sipping warm tea and chicken broth heated on her small burner. She was concerned that she wasn't able to check the audition list at the conservatory, but she felt too sick to go, especially since the weather was miserable.

One day there was a knock on the door, and Mrs. Sombey, the landlady, stuck her head in.

"Well, miss, you're lookin' much better today," she remarked as she entered. "I dare say you'll be up and around in no time. Brought you today's mail. You've got a letter. Looks like it's from Arkansas."

Laurel propped herself up in bed, the quilt jumbled around her, hoping it might be from Mr. Fordyce, to whom she had written twice.

After Mrs. Sombey left, Laurel tore open the envelope. Inside was a check and a brief note:

March 12, 1901

Laurel, you'll need something to live on while you're in Boston.
I'll send you a check like this each month.

Papa Lee

She reread the note and studied the amount on the check. Should she accept it? She certainly needed the money. This was just like Papa Lee. He had always been so generous, always giving her things. This was his way of reaching out to her, and Laurel knew it.

At that thought, Laurel blew her nose with a handkerchief and looked around her sparsely furnished room. A single overstuffed chair sat in one corner beside a table that held the small burner she had purchased in a secondhand store.

How different this was from her room at the Woodwards! Laurel thought about the polished maple furniture, the armoire filled with beautiful clothes, the white ruffled curtains, and her big four-poster bed piled high with pillows. She remembered the house in detail. There was the kitchen with Ella bustling about, the front hall with the Queen Anne table, and the side porch with white wicker furniture and flowered cushions. And, of course, there was the parlor where she had spent so many enjoyable hours playing the piano and singing.

Her mind wandered into Dr. Lee's office behind the house. She could see beyond its quaint waiting room to Dr. Lee at his desk, his stethoscope still hanging around his neck. She imagined herself sitting on the front porch swing waiting for him to get home from making house calls. She wandered into Mother's sitting room and saw Ava look up from her embroidery with a tender, welcoming smile.

Laurel shook her head. No, she mustn't allow her momentary homesickness to blot out her reason for coming to Boston. Even if life in Boston was not turning out at all like she had expected, she knew there was a purpose to it all.

On the first day she felt well enough to get out, Laurel went to the conservatory to check the audition list. To her dismay, she saw she had missed her scheduled audition. She had waited all this time and now, because of her cold, she had missed her chance.

However, as she pushed open the heavy front door, after her first disappointment, Laurel felt an odd and unexpected sense of relief sweep over her. Maybe she really wasn't ready. It would be far worse to try and fail. As the door shut behind her, she realized that this delay would give her time to find a coach.

To Laurel's delight, the ad she had placed in the newspaper brought immediate response. A number of Boston's well-to-do mothers were looking for someone to teach piano to their children in their homes. At first Laurel was thrilled, but she soon realized that teaching music in her pupils' homes meant hours on the trolleys, on trams, and on foot. She also discovered that teaching was not always fun. Listening over and over to clumsy little fingers stumbling over scales sometimes made her feel like running away. Yet it was a price she was willing to pay. She was beginning to save money for a coach.

The chilly Massachusetts spring soon turned into a hot summer. Humid days were followed by breathless nights when the air barely stirred the thin lace curtains in her bedroom windows. To make matters worse, several of her pupils canceled their lessons to vacation with their families at second homes at Cape Cod or on the coast of Maine. With less traveling and teaching to take up her day, Laurel had more time to think about contacting Mrs. Maynard.

One Saturday in June, she finally went to see Wembley Square, the address for Mrs. Bennett Maynard. She took a trolley to the end of the line, then at the direction of the conductor, walked another few blocks. She strolled under tall, shady elms along quiet streets lined with impressive homes set well back from the boulevard.

Laurel walked slowly, looking for the house number she had seen in the newspaper. All at once she saw it! Number 1573. It was displayed on a polished brass plaque set among climbing ivy in the post of a brick wall. The house was a stately pink brick structure with black shutters. Curved double steps with iron railing led up to a paneled front door.

For a long time, Laurel observed it. How different this brick mansion looked from the picket fences and neat frame houses in Meadowridge. There was no sign of life, either on the street or behind the large windows. Did the family go to Maine or Martha's Vineyard for summer vacation like a lot of other well-to-do Boston families?

Laurel wished she knew.

Yet, what would she say to Mrs. Maynard? She really wasn't ready to meet her somehow, even though she had rehearsed a conversation in her mind over and over. Laurel finally boarded the trolley. Her mind asked the question, What should her next step be?

16

Glad to see her favorite small table in the corner at Pasquini's Restaurant empty, Laurel seated herself, picked up the menu, and looked at it. She couldn't seem to read it, distracted as she was by thoughts of where she had been that afternoon.

The guarded iron fences and well-trimmed boxwood hedges had cast a strange spell on her. She tried to imagine the beautiful dark-haired girl in her locket living in that home, hopping into a stately carriage or drinking afternoon tea in the sunroom. Then she saw Mrs. Campbell's shabby boardinghouse. What was it like for her mother to live in a flat like that after being raised in such luxury and comfort? Laurel had never heard her mother complain, not even when her living conditions had brought on the illness that caused her death.

"I recommend the lasagna tonight." A male voice interrupted her thoughts.

Startled, Laurel looked up. Her waiter was the same young man she had encountered twice before. She stared at him.

His smile widened. "To answer your question, yes, I'm a student at the conservatory. I work here part-time to support myself and my voice coach."

Laurel felt her cheeks flush.

"Oh, well, I—" she stammered. "I'm sorry, I didn't—"

"Don't apologize, please." His dark eyes sparkled. "Most of us have to work while we attend the conservatory. Surely there's not such a thing as an artist who doesn't have to struggle, is there?" He pulled out his writing pad. "Now, what about you? What would you like for dinner?"

Flustered, Laurel looked down at the menu.

"May I make a suggestion?" he continued. "I've sampled the minestrone soup and found it to be delicious. Or maybe something lighter since it's so warm outside today. Although, the lasagna is delicious and a fresh green salad would make it perfect."

The man paused and cocked his dark curly head to one side. "Even though we've met before, may I introduce myself formally?" He gave a small bow. "My name is Gene Michela."

"I'm Laurel Vestal."

"Am I correct in assuming you're also a student at the conservatory?"

"Well, not exactly. At least, not yet. That is, I haven't been accepted." Laurel shrugged her shoulders. "I missed my audition, and now I've discovered I need a coach. So I've been giving piano lessons to earn the money—"

Suddenly, Laurel stopped. Why was she talking so much, telling all of this to a waiter?

"Oh, dear!" she exclaimed. "I don't know what I'm saying, I mean, I don't know what I want to eat—" She closed the menu and handed it back to him.

"I'm sorry. I didn't mean to rush you. Would you like some time to decide? Perhaps you'd like a refreshing glass of lemonade while you're deciding?"

"That would be nice," she murmured, still blushing.

By the time he was back, she had managed to recover her composure.

"I've consulted Mario, the chef, and he suggests a perfect selection for this summer evening." The waiter whisked a tall frosty glass off the tray and set it in front of her. "A combination plate of chilled asparagus, fresh tomatoes, cucumbers, cheese, and bread. May I bring it out for you?"

Dazzled by the attention, the girl simply nodded. Secretly, she hoped this choice wouldn't make it necessary for her to eat crackers and oranges in her room for the rest of the week.

As she finished her supper, Gene appeared again, this time with a chilled dish of pistachio ice cream and a thin chocolate wafer. "Compliments of the chef!" He set it down on a small, round, lace paper doily.

There was nothing for her to do but eat the ice cream. She hadn't enjoyed such a luxury in a very long time. It reminded her of summer days with the gang at home, eating ice cream at the Meadowridge Parlor after tennis or croquet.

Gene reappeared with her check on a small tray, then stood behind her chair as she rose. Laurel thanked him and moved over to the cash register. He waited while she paid, then escorted her to the door.

"It was a pleasure serving you, Miss Vestal," he said as he opened the door for her with a little bow. "I hope we meet again."

It wasn't until Laurel was back on the sidewalk and had counted her change that she realized neither the lemonade nor the pistachio ice cream had been included on the bill.

"Miss Vestal! Miss Vestal!" She was halfway down the block when she heard her name.

She turned to see Gene Michela sprinting after her. Had she forgotten something?

"Miss Vestal," he panted, "I beg your pardon if this seems too personal, but do you attend church?"

Startled, she nodded her head, her dark curls blowing in an unexpected summer breeze. "Yes, I do, but I haven't since coming to Boston."

His voice had calmed down now. "What I meant was I'm singing at a wedding next Saturday afternoon at four o'clock." He held out a small card. "It would be perfectly all right if you slipped in the side door and sat in the back." He smiled shyly. "I'd like for you to come, if you have no other plans."

"Well, I'll try," she replied as she looked down at the card he had handed her.

"Oh, yes, do try!" He smiled. "I'll sing as if you were there anyway."

Then he backed away a few steps. "I've got to get back to the restaurant. Good-bye." With a wave of his hand, he ran back down the sidewalk.

On the following Saturday, a little before three o'clock, Laurel found herself entering the side door of an old Boston church. It was tall and stately, set back from the street and surrounded by an iron fence. This was completely different from the small, white frame Meadowridge Church she knew so well.

The interior was dim and quiet. Down the long aisle to the front of the church, about ten pews had white satin ribbons. Feeling like an intruder, Laurel found a seat in the rear shielded by one of the big stone pillars. She gazed at the arched stained-glass windows. Sunlight slanted through, leaving scattered colors. Each window showed an event in Jesus' ministry. One was the feeding of the multitude, another the Good Shepherd. Artistic and beautiful, the windows brought the Bible stories to life.

Then, Laurel drew in a breath. A third window showed Jesus with the little children. She had seen this window before. But where? And when? Evidence of a life gone by seemed to float across her mind like a butterfly. Here in Boston everything seemed to link her to her past. Maybe everything *was* leading her back to her roots, her family, her identity.

Suddenly, the deep tones of the organ reverberated through the empty church. With a start, Laurel listened as the organist tested his music for the wedding. She thought about Sunday school in Meadowridge and her friends, Toddy and Kit. She wondered how they were doing. She missed her two dearest friends. Would she ever find a friend here in Boston?

A short while later, the wedding began. A few minutes before the bride entered, a rich tenor voice filled the entire building. Its deep sound was glorious. Laurel felt tiny prickles spread along her scalp and down her spine. It was Gene. There was more than surface charm to this young man. His gift was truly God given.

Tears welled up in her eyes. Sitting in this sanctuary, seeing the window, and hearing Gene's beautiful voice had been an emotional experience. Before the ceremony was over, she rose quietly and left.

17

Over the next few weeks, Laurel was continually drawn back to Wembley Square and the Maynard mansion. She would sit on one of the benches in the shady park across the boulevard. Was this her mother's family home, and was this the grandmother she had never met? If so, why had she not searched for her missing daughter? Did she even know she had a granddaughter? What had her mama meant when she had said that Laurel would meet her grandmother someday, when all is forgiven? Questions tumbled over and over in her mind, questions she yearned to answer but couldn't.

June quickly passed into July and August. Still the house showed no sign of activity. Laurel determined she would contact this Mrs. Maynard upon her return. She did not want to shock her, so she decided to send flowers and a note first, introducing herself and asking if she might call. Then, with her parents' marriage license and her birth certificate, she would go to the house to see her.

Laurel fingered the tiny heart locket still hanging around her neck. Many of the lost fragments of her background were still missing. How had her parents met?

Why had a young widow from a wealthy Boston family chosen not to go back to her family? What deep secret kept her away? Would Laurel ever find out? Was this Mrs. Maynard the most important missing piece of the puzzle?

Soon it would be time to apply to the conservatory. Knowing that new schedules for classes and auditions would soon be posted, Laurel walked to the school one day. In the administration office, she filled out the forms, but the question of who would be responsible for her tuition stopped her. She did not want to write in Dr. Woodward's name. With a sigh, she shoved all the papers into her carrying case and decided to think everything over before completing her application.

After explaining this to the woman behind the desk, Laurel opened the office door. As she did, she accidentally bumped into someone and dropped her case on the floor. The forms and sheets of music flew everywhere.

"Miss Vestal! Don't you ever look where you're going?"

It was Gene Michela!

"Mr. Michela! I'm so sorry," she said, bending down again to pick up the scattered papers.

This time, Gene bent down to help her and the two bumped heads. They collapsed into helpless laughter. Then their eyes met. Laurel felt a strange recognition, as though she were looking into the eyes of an old friend, someone she had known for a long time. She had never experienced this feeling before. It was as if a beautiful bridge had suddenly been built connecting her to him, a bridge she was crossing without having taken a step.

All Laurel's girlish dreams of falling in love came into focus. She had held onto the secret hope that someday she would meet that special someone. Was Gene that person?

"It's good to see you again, Miss Vestal, or should I say, *bump* into you." Gene's dark eyes danced with mischief as he looked at her.

"I'm not always so clumsy, believe it or not," Laurel laughed. She tied the strap around her portfolio, then added shyly, "I heard you sing."

"Did you?" He sounded pleased. "I so hoped you would."

"You are very good, you know." She looked at him directly. "You really have to sing, don't you?"

"It's my life!" he exclaimed.

"It shows."

They left the administration office and walked down the long hallway together. Other students passed by, but Laurel was aware of only him.

Once outside, Gene suggested they sit down on the steps in the sunshine. He told her he had just returned from a month's tour with a choral group.

"It gave me a taste of what a concert singer's life would be like. You're on the road two weeks at a time, trying to sleep sitting up on a day coach." The man shook his head. "Staying at run-down hotels, eating terrible food!" He laughed. "For an Italian boy, this is the worst."

He changed the subject. "Speaking of food, I'm hungry. How about you?"

It was well past noon, and Laurel realized her breakfast of wheat crackers and tea had been long ago.

"Come on." Gene stood up and held out his hand. "Let's go get a frankfurter."

At the park's concession stand, a ruddy-faced man in a limp chef's cap and apron took their order. He forked sizzling wieners into long buns, then slathered them with mustard.

"My treat!" Gene held up his hand as Laurel opened her purse. "Not that the menu is elegant, but just wait until I have my debut at La Scala! Then we'll really celebrate."

Laurel thrilled at his excitement. He wanted to perform at the famous Italian opera house, and he wanted her to celebrate with him!

Laurel held their frankfurters while Gene bought two bottles of soda. The couple found a bench and sat down to eat. After they had finished, they walked along a stone path bordered by colorful flowers down to a small lake. Gene took off his plaid jacket and spread it on the grass for Laurel to sit down. Deep in conversation, the two went on talking as though they had known each other for a long time.

Suddenly Gene scrambled to his feet. "Laurel, I'm sorry. I didn't realize it was getting so late. I'd like to walk you home, but I won't make it to work on time."

"Then maybe I'll see you later at the restaurant," she replied shyly.

"Oh, that is a second job. I'm filling in for the regular waiter who's been sick." He seemed embarrassed. "I could make up something that would impress you, but the truth is I'm a night watchman at a warehouse."

"Oh, Gene, you don't have to try to impress me."

"You're right. My father always says all work is noble as long as it's honest."

"I believe that too," she declared.

"But I did intend to take you home." A frown appeared across his brow. "I don't even know where you live. And I don't know how to get in touch with you again."

He was already moving away, walking backwards as he spoke. "Could we meet again?" he asked boldly. "Maybe here? Tomorrow afternoon?"

"Yes!" Laurel called out. "Tomorrow afternoon. Right here."

Gene waved his hand, turned, and made a run for it. She watched him until his figure faded in the distance. How wild this was! And how happy she felt.

Laurel picked up her music portfolio and strolled toward the trolley stop. She was still smiling when she got off at her stop. Yes, this had been the happiest day she had ever known.

The next afternoon, her new friend was in the park waiting for her beside the small playground. Sounds of children swinging and laughing reached Laurel's ears. Two mothers were talking on a nearby park bench, while a third rocked her baby buggy back and forth to quiet a fussy infant.

When Gene saw her coming, he broke into a big smile.

"Laurel! I'm so glad to see you." He rushed up to her and held out both hands. "To tell you the truth, I thought I'd dreamed the whole thing." He threw back his head and laughed. "And then last night I kept kicking myself for not ditching the job and seeing you right to your doorstep. I was afraid you thought I'd been rude and had changed your mind about seeing me."

Laurel shook her head. "Of course not. I told you I understood. Really!"

"Sure?"

"Positive. I wouldn't have come if I hadn't wanted to."

"Truthfully?"

"Yes, truthfully. Don't you believe me?"

"I do." He squeezed her hands gently, feeling the softness of her skin. "Let's always promise to tell each other the truth, no matter what," he added earnestly.

Laurel nodded in agreement. *Always?* Did he mean there was a future they would share?

As they talked, Gene realized his heart was pounding so hard in his chest it felt as if he had been running. What was it about this young woman that attracted him so? Her long dark curls flowed in ringlets about her shoulders, and her small nose crinkled when she laughed. He noticed her smooth slender neck above the ruffled edge of her high-necked white blouse. She was beautiful.

The rest of the afternoon flew by again. The two young people never seemed to run out of things to talk about. Laurel discovered that Gene had a wonderful sense of humor. Everything that had ever happened to him turned into a humorous or exciting story. In some ways, he reminded her of Papa Lee, who could do the same thing.

By the end of the second day, Laurel knew a great deal more about Gene. He had grown up in a small town on the coast of New England. Unlike Laurel, he was part of a large, close Italian family with grandparents, uncles, aunts, and cousins. Although most of his relatives were fishermen, they were proud of his choice of a singing career. He had won a scholarship to the conservatory and had come to Boston right out of high school. In spite of the fact that his tuition was paid, he still had to work part-time as a night watchman to support himself and pay for his rent as well as his voice teacher. The owners of the restaurant, the Pasquinis, were old family friends. They had taken Gene under their wing, feeding him and giving him the temporary second job as a waiter.

"Do you have a coach?" he asked Laurel as they sat on a bench watching some squirrels scamper up and down a tree.

"No, not yet. I suppose I'll have to get one." She hesitated. "I really haven't done much about preparing for my audition either. I just don't know—"

Gene looked puzzled. "I don't understand what you mean."

To her surprise, that day Laurel found herself confiding in him. She shared her story and before she knew it had told him the real reason for her move.

"I never really thought seriously about studying voice," she said. "But when my high school music teacher brought it up, it seemed like a good excuse to do what I'd been secretly planning all these years."

"Have you found out about your real family yet?"

Laurel told him what she knew. "I've found my grandmother, or at least the person I think is my grandmother, and I want to try to see her. I'm a little afraid, I guess."

"Would you like me to go with you when the time comes?"

Gene's offer touched Laurel deeply, but she shook her head no. She had to do this alone.

18

As the weeks went by, the couple saw each other nearly every day, spending the afternoons strolling or sitting together in the park. Within a short time, being with Gene was the highlight of Laurel's day. She was happier than she had ever imagined possible.

Gene had come from a large, loving family. He was outgoing, optimistic, and enthusiastic. His personality complemented hers in every way. He had ambition and was willing to work hard to achieve his goals, determined not to let anything stop him. He believed everything happened for a purpose and that God had a plan for each person's life.

"Like our meeting the way we did," he told her one afternoon as they were walking hand in hand down the sidewalk near the restaurant. "There was a reason for it. Nothing is an accident."

He continued. "God gave me a voice, Laurel, so I could make a living. But I'm supposed to do more. I'm supposed to contribute something to other people's lives too."

The scent of freshly baked bread floated by as they passed a small bakery.

"I'm never happier than when I'm singing. That's how I know I'm fulfilling God's purpose for me."

Laurel had never thought about life this way before. She wondered if what Gene was saying was true. Did God have a purpose for her life? She wanted to believe it because Gene had told her so, but doubts continued to cross her mind. And then something happened.

Even though Dr. Lee continued to send a monthly check, Laurel felt guilty whenever she cashed them. She felt she should be supporting herself, especially since she had gone against the Woodwards' wishes. She decided to find a job that would give her a regular income. Then she could afford a voice coach and apply to the conservatory.

One day she was taking a shortcut back from the park to her rooming house when she passed a music store. She noticed the sign HELP WANTED, PIANIST in the front window. On impulse, the young woman entered the store to ask about the sign.

"Yes, we're looking for someone to play the sheet music we sell to customers," replied the gentleman, looking at her over his glasses. "Are you interested?"

"Yes, sir, I am," she answered politely.

"Well, then, why don't you play a few pieces for me? My name is Mr. Jacobsen. I am the owner of the store."

Something about the man's kind eyes and snowy hair reminded her of Dr. Lee. She instantly felt at ease. After she had sight-read several pieces, the owner hired her on the spot.

Laurel could not wait to tell Gene the good news. That evening at Pasquini's, he congratulated her heartily and then told her he had some news of his own.

"Actually, both good news and bad," he said as they sat at the corner table.

"What do you mean?" Laurel felt a spurt of alarm.

"Don't look so worried," Gene reassured her. "The good news is I have a new job, a singing job. It's just in the chorus, but at least I'll be singing."

"That's wonderful, Gene!"

"Wait until you hear the rest," he cautioned. "It's a late summer theater production of Gilbert and Sullivan's *The Pirates of Penzance*. And it's at the Cape."

Laurel felt her heart sink. She tried not to show it. "Cape Cod?"

"Yes. I'll be away until the fall. But after this, I'll have a chance to try out for another one."

Laurel quickly took a sip of water. She could feel an old feeling rising within her. She recognized it as abandonment.

"I hate the idea of being away from you, Laurel, but I can't turn down this chance."

"You're right, Gene. You can't." Laurel tried to look on the bright side as she traced the small squares on the red checkered tablecloth with her finger. "It's only a few weeks."

"That's right. The time will pass quickly." He reached for her hand. "We have today and Friday. I don't have to be there until Monday morning, so I can leave Sunday on the morning train."

Laurel looked at him fondly, knowing how much she would miss him.

"We'll go to the concert in the park on Saturday?" he suggested.

"Perfect," she replied.

Saturday afternoon, Laurel dressed as if she were going to a ball. She chose an outfit Mrs. Danby, the Meadowridge seamstress, had made for her last summer—a short yellow cotton jacket edged with embroidery, a delicate yellow blouse, and a flared skirt. Her broad-brimmed straw hat, perfect for shading her delicate skin from the sun, completed the outfit.

At her first sight of Gene strolling up the sidewalk toward the boardinghouse, something tugged at her heart. Right then she knew she had fallen in love.

When he saw her, he struck a dramatic pose, declaring theatrically, "What a vision you are! I should have brought you flowers!"

"Flowers?"

"Yes, of course. Flowers are the accepted gift of courtship, are they not?" Gene held up a basket. "Instead, I bring *food!*" he said with an Italian accent. "Thanks to Mrs. Pasquini, who packed us a lunch you won't believe."

"Come on then," Laurel said merrily. "Let's go enjoy it."

At the park, they roamed over the rolling hills dotted with lovely old trees near the amphitheater, where the orchestra would assemble later for the program. When they finally found a spot, Gene opened the large wicker basket. With great flare, he pulled out a small green rug and spread it on the grass, tossing two fluffy red pillows on top of it. Next came a blue checkered tablecloth, plates, napkins, and silverware.

Laurel's eyes widened as she watched him unpack the food. "My goodness, you were right," she exclaimed as he set out the platters. "This is a lot of food!"

Mrs. Pasquini had fixed a platter of thinly sliced ham with squares of cheese. She had sent small containers filled with black olives, pasta salad, cherry tomatoes, sliced cucumbers, and fresh fruit. A twisted loaf of crusty homemade bread topped off the banquet.

"Well, you don't have to eat if you don't want to," Gene teased as he poured her a cup of chilled lemonade.

"Oh, I'll force myself!" Laurel smiled, dipping a tiny tomato in some dilled mayonnaise. This was a welcome change from the limited diet she'd been living on the past weeks.

They ate and talked and laughed, completely relaxed and happy in each other's company. Laurel tried not to think that the next day Gene would be going away. Every time a thought threatened to spoil things, she pushed it to the back of her mind. There would be time enough to miss him when he was gone. Now, she would just enjoy him.

"What will you have for dessert, madam?" Gene held up a bunch of glistening purple grapes in one hand and a round blushed peach in the palm of the other.

"Oh, I don't know, Gene, I'm so full now." Laurel patted her green cummerbund. "Why don't we share a peach?"

"No sooner said than done," the host said as he cut the fruit in two, removed the pit, and handed her one half.

"Oh, it's so juicy!" she laughed. She tried to capture the sweet juice with her tongue as it ran down her chin.

Gene leaned forward and gently wiped her mouth and chin with a white handkerchief. He was so close Laurel could see his thick eyelashes shadowing his brown eyes.

"Oh, Laurel, I can't remember what my life was like before I met you," he said.

She caught her breath. "I know. I feel the same way."

"I don't want this ever to end," he whispered. "Sometimes when I'm with you, I think I hear bells ringing and music playing."

"Me too, Gene," Laurel sighed.

Gene grinned. "Then again, maybe it's the orchestra tuning up their instruments." He stood up and took her hand. "Let's gather our belongings and move closer."

The sky had turned a deep blue, and a faint first star had appeared by the time they were settled. Soon a white-haired conductor marched on stage to the podium and rapped his baton. The first strains of Vivaldi's *Four Seasons* rose into the evening air.

After the concert, on the trolley ride back to the boardinghouse, they held hands, still caught up in the beautiful music. They got off the trolley and walked the last block very slowly. At the corner, Gene drew Laurel away from the circle of light shining from the lamppost into the shadows and took her into his arms. His cheek rested on hers and she heard him whisper her name. She closed her eyes as he kissed her.

"Laurel, I love you," he told her quietly. "But I have nothing to offer you. I'm as poor as a church mouse. I barely make enough to pay room and board, even with my scholarship—"

Laurel placed her fingers on his lips, shutting off the flow of his words. Then she put her arms around his lean neck. A tenderness filled her heart.

"It doesn't matter, Gene. I'm poor too. But we'll both make it." Gene looked deep into her eyes as she whispered, "We'll help each other. It'll take time, but we're young. We have all the time in the world!"

The week after Gene left seemed empty. Laurel continued her job at Jacobsen's Music Store. She enjoyed meeting and talking with the different buyers who came in. When they were interested in a particular song, Laurel would play it for them on the piano. Mr. Jacobsen seemed pleased with her work.

On her half day off, she decided to travel out to the neighborhood where Mrs. Maynard lived. To her surprise, a gardener was clipping the thick boxwood hedge while a man on a ladder was washing the outside of the downstairs windows. The sight of the activity excited her as she stood beside the iron fence. She quickly realized the family was home.

The next day, she ordered a flower arrangement of daisies, her mother's favorite flower. It was to be delivered to the house at Wembley Square. Laurel placed a note with it.

August 15, 1901

Dear Mrs. Maynard:

I am writing you because I believe we are related. I am the daughter of Lillian Maynard and Paul Vestal, born in this city

September 1882. If you would be so gracious to receive me, I would like to call on you to discuss this further.

Sincerely,
Laurel Elaine Vestal

Underneath her signature, she put the address of Mrs. Sombey's rooming house.

A week dragged by. Every day Laurel hurried home from the music store hoping to receive a reply. By the end of the week, Laurel was convinced the lady wasn't going to reply at all. At this point she made an important decision.

Dressed in a dove-gray linen suit and straw hat ringed with white daisies, Laurel stood at the mirror. She fingered the chain of her gold locket. Would Mrs. Maynard receive her? Whatever happened, she would not put off making her grandmother aware of her existence.

She carefully pulled on white cotton gloves and picked up her handbag containing the envelope with the copies of her parents' marriage certificate and her birth certificate. With some trepidation she took the trolley out to the quiet neighborhood, not knowing what awaited her.

Laurel mounted the steps of the impressive house and lifted the polished knocker on the front door.

A gray-haired butler opened the door and regarded her coldly.

"Is Mrs. Maynard in?"

He held out a small silver tray. "Your card, miss."

"I have no card," she replied.

"Then whom shall I say is calling?" he asked suspiciously.

"Miss Laurel Vestal."

"One moment, miss."

Laurel slipped inside the front door before he could close it. The butler turned sharply on his heels and disappeared down a long hall toward a closed door. She could hear his knock before he entered.

Left alone, she looked around her. The foyer was oval with a parquet floor. A runner of dark red carpeting extended from the front door up a broad staircase to the second floor. At the curve of the upstairs balcony, the pale light of the sun shined through a stained-glass window.

A few minutes later, the butler returned.

"Although this is not Mrs. Maynard's regular day for receiving visitors, she will see you." The man's tone was icy. "Come this way, please."

Laurel clutched her handbag tightly and followed the man down the hall. Part of her wanted to run away, but she remembered to be strong and of good courage. The Lord was with her.

"Miss Vestal, madam," the butler announced as he stepped back for Laurel to pass.

The room had gold-framed portraits on paneled walls, heavy carved furniture, and a thick Oriental carpet. Laurel found three people in the room rather than the one she had expected. Laurel's hand tightened around her purse, the proof of her heritage securely tucked inside.

One of them, a man dressed in a navy suit, got to his feet and moved slowly behind the chair of one of the women. He eyed her with curiosity. The two elegantly dressed elderly women sat in matching armchairs beside one another. Laurel wondered which one of them was Mrs. Maynard.

"Mrs. Maynard?" Laurel's voice sounded timid but steady.

There was silence. The man shifted from one foot to the other. Finally, one of the women spoke.

"I'm Mrs. Maynard."

The speaker was a thin woman with fine features. She had an aristocratic nose, erect posture, and beautifully styled iron-gray hair. She gestured to the others. "This is my cousin, Mrs. Farraday, and her son, Ormond."

The man acknowledged the introduction with a nod. Mrs. Farraday merely stared at Laurel, her expression blank.

"You wished to see me?" Mrs. Maynard spoke in a cultured New England accent.

"I am Laurel Vestal, Mrs. Maynard. You may recall I wrote to you a week ago, asking if I might call?" She tried to keep her voice from shaking and hoped they wouldn't detect how nervous she was. When Mrs. Maynard did not reply, she persisted, "You did receive my note, didn't you?"

The elderly woman tilted her head slightly but did not speak. Laurel could feel the tension mounting in the room. She rushed on. "I've been waiting for an answer. When I didn't hear from you, I decided to come in person."

"The very idea!" the other woman gasped.

Laurel froze. Had she committed some terrible social blunder? Well, it was too late to worry about that now. She squared her shoulders. She had come for some confirmation of who she believed herself to be, and she would stay until she received an answer.

Mrs. Maynard laid a hand on her cousin's arm. "Gertrude, please. I'll handle this. Would you care to sit down, Miss Vestal?"

"Perhaps I should come back at a more convenient time?" Laurel said, thinking the confrontation would be better when the two of them were alone.

Mrs. Maynard rose from her chair. "Yes, perhaps that would be best. We are due at a meeting of the Symphony Society very shortly."

"Would you care to give me another day and time?"

Mrs. Maynard moved stiffly toward the door to usher her out. "I will send word when that can be arranged."

At the door, Laurel drew out the envelope containing the copies of the certificates and handed it to her. "In the meantime, Mrs. Maynard, perhaps you will find these interesting."

The thin controlled mouth quivered slightly. There was a second's pause before Mrs. Maynard took the envelope.

Outside in the warm summer afternoon the bright sunshine made Laurel dizzy after the dim interior of the Maynard house. Laurel took in a deep breath and leaned against the brick wall.

It was done! She had carried out her part. The rest was up to Mrs. Maynard.

20

When she returned to the boardinghouse, Laurel discovered a letter from Gene waiting for her. She ran upstairs to her room, tore open the envelope, and devoured every word. The note was short and contained an unexpected message.

Laurel,

I am making a quick trip to Boston. Will be there early Sunday morning. I have a surprise for you!

Love, Gene

The thought of Gene's arrival brightened her mood. During the next week, Laurel heard nothing from Mrs. Maynard. Maybe it was her own fault. Her expectations about meeting her grandmother had been high. She had wanted Mrs. Maynard to be the one, but now she wasn't as sure. "When all is forgiven . . ." That phrase still haunted her. What did it mean? Maybe it was too late.

On Saturday night, Laurel's thoughts turned to Gene. He had been away for nearly three weeks now. What if he had found someone else among the pretty actresses and singers in the cast? He was attractive and talented. But that was silly—just part of the uncertainty she felt after her disappointing visit with Mrs. Maynard.

Sunday morning, dressed in a pink linen dress that was one of Gene's favorites, she posted herself at the bedroom window to watch for him.

As soon as Laurel spotted him coming down the street carrying a brown paper package, she flew down the stairs and slipped out the front door. She was waiting for him at the top of the porch steps when he came through the gate.

With his foot on the first step, Gene looked up at her, smiling. Her heart melted. Any doubts about pretty actresses faded when she saw the tenderness in his eyes.

"Hello, Laurel," he greeted her softly as she came down the steps toward him. "I've missed you."

"I've missed you too, Gene."

"Then no one stole you away from me while I was gone?"

Laurel laughed and shook her head. She might have asked him the same question, if she hadn't felt the love in his glance.

"Let's walk over to the park where we can find some privacy," he said, tucking her hand through his arm. "I want to tell you something."

At the park, they found their bench and sat down. Gene placed the package in her lap. "Go ahead, open it," he directed, watching her eagerly.

"What is it, Gene? You shouldn't be spending your money on presents for me." Laurel's fingers tugged at the knotted string.

"Just open it." Impatient, he whipped out his pocketknife and cut the string. "There!" he said as Laurel tore away the paper.

For a minute, she just stared. Slowly she put both her hands on either side of the narrow wood frame and lifted the picture from the box. It was a painting of a woman and her child on a beach. A wide-brimmed straw hat shadowed the woman's face. She held a parasol with one hand while extending her other toward the little girl, who was building a mound in the sand. In the lower right-hand corner were tiny initials and a date: PV/84.

Gene urged softly, "Turn it over, Laurel."

These words had been brushed on the back: August 1884, Lil and Baby L. at C.C.

Laurel's deep brown eyes filled with tears. "Where did you find this?" She looked at Gene.

"In a little art gallery on Martha's Vineyard. I was wandering around one afternoon when we didn't have rehearsal. Actually, I was looking for a gift for you. Then I saw this in the window. When I looked closely, I spotted the initials. I felt sure it was one of your father's paintings."

"Oh, Gene, I'm sure it is," she exclaimed. "Do you suppose there are more?"

"I intend to go back and find out." He held the brown paper wrapping in his lap so it wouldn't blow away. "The new owner of the shop has stacks of unframed canvases in a storage shed behind the shop. He hasn't had time to sort through them yet. He says this is one of the finest examples of Impressionist paintings he's seen in a long time."

Laurel's mind wandered quickly back in time. She could see the painting of the lighthouse hanging over her mother's piano in Mrs. Campbell's boardinghouse.

"The style is like the painting that hung over our piano when I was a little girl, Gene," Laurel explained. "The same sky and sand and feeling of lightness." She gently placed the canvas back in the box. "When I asked Mama why Papa painted a seascape, she told me that every summer a group of their artist friends would rent a house at Cape Cod. Papa loved painting the scenery there."

"Then we may be on to something. When I told this fellow I knew the daughter of the artist, he told me he'd get in touch with you when he'd had a chance to look through the shed. He seemed to think your father's work might be very valuable."

"Gene, how can I ever thank you?" Laurel asked as she began wrapping the box.

"Seeing you happy is all the thanks I need." Gene took the package from her and retied the strings. "In fact, I want to spend the rest of my life making you happy."

Laurel held her breath, not daring to speak.

"I love you, Laurel," Gene said. "I think I knew it from the first day. Would you—Do you—" he hesitated.

"We'll work it out, my darling," Laurel's voice chimed in.

After they had kissed, Gene jumped to his feet and tossed his cap in the air. "I'm the happiest guy in Boston!" he yelled as he caught the spinning hat.

"Oh, Gene!" Laurel smiled.

"I'm also the hungriest! Come on, let's go get some breakfast."

Late that afternoon, Laurel went to the train station to see Gene off again.

"No more of these partings," he told her. "I have enough money now to last me through the next semester at the conservatory. I'm not going to take any more jobs that mean going out of town."

At the sound of a whistle, Gene took her hands. "I want us to be married, Laurel, as soon as possible. We'll manage somehow."

"I have my job, and Mr. Jacobsen has talked about giving me a raise."

Gene's handsome face became very serious. "What about your plans to attend the conservatory?"

"Gene, I've realized over these past few months that I don't have the same burning desire to sing like you do." Laurel raised her voice over the hustle and bustle around them. "I love music. I enjoy playing and singing, but it isn't the focus of my life."

"All aboard!" The conductor's words crossed the platform as steam hissed and the gears of the locomotive began to grind.

Gene released her hands. "I must go," he said. "See you in two weeks!"

21

Two days later, Laurel ran her fingers lightly over the canvas, feeling the rough brush strokes. Looking at it, she could almost feel the warm grains of the sand under her feet. Strangely, the painting felt real to her. It was almost as if she were there. Somewhere way back in her mind she could smell the salty scent of the sea breeze as it bent the tall dune grass behind the figure of the mother. She could see the cloudless blue sky and the sun-washed roof of the weathered shingled cottage in the distance.

It was all a miracle. She ticked off the events that had brought this painting into her possession. She had come to Boston to trace her heritage. She had bumped into Gene on the steps of the conservatory. She had eaten at Pasquini's. The couple had collided in the administration office. Gene had happened to be on Martha's Vineyard and happened on the art gallery, where the painting happened to be on display. It all flowed together somehow.

Laurel thought of Gene with longing. She was proud he had been selected to perform in the opera, but she missed him terribly.

The next day when Laurel came in from work, Mrs. Sombey was waiting for her. Her eyes were dancing with curiosity.

"This came for you today, Miss Vestal." She handed Laurel an envelope written in fine script. "A stylish carriage drove up and stopped right out front! Then a driver in a dark blue coat come right up to the door. He asked if this was where Miss Laurel Vestal lived. Of course, I says it was. Then he handed me that envelope." The landlady's cheeks were flushed. "Why, look there at the red wax seal!"

"Thank you so much, Mrs. Sombey." Laurel started up the stairway.

"Ain't you going to see who it's from?"

"Yes, ma'am, in just a minute," she called back over her shoulder.

As soon as she had shut the door and put down her bag, she ripped open the envelope.

September 1, 1901

My dear Miss Vestal,

I have cleared my social calendar and will be at home Monday next from three to five in the afternoon if you would care to call.

Cordially,
Elaine Maynard

Elaine! Her first name was Elaine! This *was* the grandmother she had been searching for! Laurel folded the note and replaced it in the fancy envelope. That evening she penned a reply, accepting the offer.

Following work the next day, Laurel discovered another letter at her door. Thinking it was from Gene, she quickly opened it. To her great surprise, this one came from Ava. Laurel sat down on her bed to read.

August 1901

My darling girl,

I should have written this letter months ago. It has taken me all this time to come to terms with my unhappiness, Laurel. I was wrong not to give you my full blessing when you left. Please forgive me. I feel like the Chinese princess in one of your favorite stories. Do you remember? She caged the bird so it wouldn't fly away, and the bird stopped singing. I love you very much, Laurel. So does Papa Lee. I want you to be happy and sing and live a full, wonderful life. So I release you from the bonds I tied around you. Be free, my darling, to be whatever you want to be. Whatever makes you happy will make us happy too.

Your loving mother,
Ava Woodward

Laurel did not move for a long time. She clutched the letter to her chest. Tears welled up in her eyes and spilled in a river down her cheeks. All the months of heartache washed away as they fell into her lap. Her parents had forgiven her. The love they had cherished was still there. Like a bird just released to fly, Laurel's heart seemed lighter now. She felt like singing. It was well with her soul.

The next day Laurel dressed with great care. She selected a dress Ava had always liked, navy blue silk with embroidered collar and cuffs. As she put on her matching straw sailor hat, she thought her mama as well as the Woodwards would have been proud of her today. She looked every inch a lady.

Unlike before, Laurel decided to ride in style this afternoon. She hailed a hackney cab and at precisely two minutes before three lifted the brass knocker. As she stood there, she looked down the street at all the other fine houses. It was very different here from the workaday world of which Laurel was a part. This place had a quiet charm. She couldn't help but wonder what her life would have been like if her grandmother had raised her here.

"Good afternoon, miss." The same butler answered the door. His tone seemed friendlier today as he stepped back and opened the door. "Mrs. Maynard will receive you in the parlor, if you will come this way."

He opened a double door leading into a small room. Laurel saw a piano in one corner, graceful chairs covered in needlepoint, a fireplace flanked by bookcases, its hearth hidden by a Japanese fan screen. Afternoon sunlight streamed through a large bay window.

"Good afternoon, Miss Vestal," Mrs. Maynard greeted the visitor from her high-back chair. She did not rise to offer her hand. She merely waved toward the opposite chair. "Do be seated."

Laurel tensed. All the confidence she had built up began to evaporate under Elaine Maynard's icy gaze. Silence stretched between them. Finally, Mrs. Maynard lifted her eyebrows and spoke.

"Well, Miss Vestal, I understand you have some reason to believe we are related."

"Yes, Mrs. Maynard," Laurel replied, trying not to fidget with her dark blue handbag. "I left you the copies of a marriage certificate and birth certificate. My mother was Lillian Maynard." Laurel's voice was growing more steady.

"My dear young lady, certainly you must know that papers can be forged. That is not proof of anything!"

Forged! Laurel was shocked. She thought she had prepared herself for any possible response. She had never even thought of this.

"I have the originals," she replied, keeping her eyes locked on Mrs. Maynard's. "They're locked in my bureau drawer."

"Did you really think I would accept this? Someone walking in here off the street?" The woman's bejeweled hands gripped the chair arms until her knuckles were white. "I have my lawyer checking your shoddy copies. What did you really hope to gain by coming here?"

Laurel could feel the anger rising into her throat. Pulling up her white gloves, she stood up.

"Mrs. Maynard, I did not come here for any reason other than to satisfy my desire to find my grandmother. My mother died nearly thirteen years ago from a disease that might have been cured. I look around here now at all this luxury and I think of the shabby little flat where we lived—"

Laurel's voice rose. "Did you ever think of your daughter all those years? Did you even know you had a granddaughter? That I was placed in an orphanage and sent on an Orphan Train out West to be adopted?"

The elderly woman slumped back in her chair. "Orphanage?"

"For two years I lived at Greystone Orphanage."

"Here in Boston?" The woman's jaw had dropped slightly now.

"Yes, only a few miles from here." Laurel drew herself up. "Mama never said a word against you and never explained what happened. Perhaps she thought I was too young. But I'm not too young now. I understand."

Laurel did not stop there. "You couldn't find it in your heart to accept the man your daughter chose to marry. You made her choose between you and him. I feel sorry for you. No, I pity you!"

"Enough!" The woman's voice was keen and sharp.

Laurel's whole body quivered, so strong were her emotions. "Don't worry. I'm going now." She headed toward the door. "If I upset you, I apologize. But I'm not sorry I came. I don't need anything you have, Mrs. Maynard. Good day."

Her hand was turning the doorknob when Mrs. Maynard's voice halted her.

"Wait! Stop! Please, Miss Vestal—Laurel—come back."

Laurel dropped her hand and slowly turned around. The older woman's face looked deathly pale, almost gray, her eyes haunted.

"You're right, my dear, Lillian Maynard was my daughter. The minute you walked in the door, I knew who you were. You look so much like her." She paused to regain her strength and catch her breath. "I must admit my cousin tried to convince me you were an imposter, and

I did have my lawyer check you out. I was hoping it wasn't true."

Mrs. Maynard toyed with the double strand of pearls about her neck. Laurel did not reply.

"You see, it was so long ago. Please sit down."

After taking a seat, Laurel removed her gloves while she listened to the story.

"Lillian was our only child, born late in our marriage. My late husband, Bennett, adored her. She was the apple of his eye, a beautiful and happy child."

The woman's voice broke. She paused a moment before she spoke again.

"That was why it was so hard to accept. She was only eighteen with her whole life ahead of her. We were planning to introduce her into Boston society with a magnificent ball. Then she told us she was in love."

Mrs. Maynard's voice grew husky. "Bennett flew into a rage, demanding to know how she had met him. We'd given her every advantage—piano lessons, voice and art lessons. And that was where she met . . . Paul Vestal.

"My husband forbade her to see him and made plans to take her away to Europe, hoping the distance would cool the romance. On the eve of our sailing date, she ran away—eloped."

The parlor was still, absolutely quiet. Laurel waited for her grandmother to continue.

"Bennett never got over it. It broke his heart and hastened his death, I'm sure. He died only a year and a half later." Mrs. Maynard sighed. "Even on his deathbed, he forbade me from trying to find her. And he made me promise I would never contact her, even after he died."

Laurel watched as tears rolled down her grandmother's wrinkled cheeks. Her heart wrenched. All the unnecessary suffering. All the pain.

"Last week my lawyer verified everything you claimed. Lillian had died in a tuberculosis sanatorium and there had been a child—" Mrs. Maynard dabbed her eyes with a lace handkerchief. "And to think, I've been on the board of Greystone Orphanage for years! Can you forgive me?"

The frail woman bowed her head and put both hands up to her face. Laurel rushed over to her. The next minute, she was hugging her grandmother for the very first time.

22

The next day, Laurel awoke to birds singing and the sun shining. She felt as content as the blue jay pruning its feathers on the tree limb just outside her window. She, Laurel Elaine Vestal, had a grandmother. She belonged. She had fulfilled her dream.

She climbed out of bed. The familiar sounds of delivery cart wheels on the cobblestone street outside floated in through the window. She pulled a sheet of stationery out of a drawer and picked up a pen before sitting down at her little round table to write.

September 10, 1901

Dearest Mother and Papa Lee,

It thrilled my heart to receive your letter. I never meant to hurt you either, but I had to come to Boston. My heart ached too, Mother. All these months I've yearned to receive your blessing and write you about all the wonderful things that are happening to me here. This past summer I met a young singer whose name is Gene Michela. Recently he asked me to marry him, and I accepted. I know you and Papa Lee will both come to love him as I do. This summer Gene found a painting at a small art shop on Martha's Vineyard. It was painted by my father, Paul Vestal. The shop owner thinks it is very valuable, so we are waiting to hear whether he has found any more of my father's work. I also recently discovered I have a grandmother who is still living. Although elderly, she lives here in Boston by herself. I'm going to visit her again today. I love you and Papa Lee so much. And I miss you both!

Your loving daughter,
Laurel

Laurel gently kissed the paper, then folded the note and inserted it into an envelope. She would drop it in the mail on her trip to Wembley Square.

A few days later, an elegant black carriage with red-rimmed wheels halted in front of the boardinghouse. A driver in a black top hat and gloves handled the handsome gray horse. The man climbed down and opened the carriage door. As Laurel stepped out, the driver bowed slightly, his black boots shining. He tipped his hat.

"Oh, Mrs. Sombey," Laurel exclaimed as she walked in the door, "I'm so glad you're here."

The landlady was flopping her feather duster along the hall table.

"I'm moving out. I have just come to get my things."

"Moving out?" Mrs. Sombey quit dusting. "Without any notice? I thought you was satisfied with your lodgings, miss."

"Oh, it's not that, Mrs. Sombey. My room has been fine. You see, I'm going to live with my grandmother on Wembley Square."

"Wembley Square?" The woman's eyes opened wide as her mouth dropped. "Your grandmother? Miss Vestal, you never said nothing about relatives in Boston."

"I know. It's really too complicated to explain." Laurel smiled. "I'll just pack my things now. My grandmother's driver is waiting for me."

As she ran up the stairs, she heard Mrs. Sombey say, "There'll be no refund, miss. If I'd known you was leaving, I could've rented that room for twice what you been payin'."

At the landing, Laurel stopped to lean over the banister. "Of course, Mrs. Sombey," she said sweetly. "I understand. I don't expect a refund."

That evening, Laurel and her grandmother had a quiet supper together before a small fire in the parlor. The food was delicious and well prepared, but neither of them ate very much.

"If you will excuse me, Laurel dear," Mrs. Maynard said, "I must retire early. I'm no longer as young as I used to be, I suppose."

"Of course, Grandmother. I understand."

She rose and passed by the cushioned chair near the bookcase where Laurel was sitting. She placed her hand on Laurel's cheek.

"At least I can look forward to many such evenings with you in the days ahead. I shall sleep peacefully, knowing my granddaughter is nearby."

With that, the elderly woman drew a yellowed envelope from her pocket. It was worn around the edges.

"I think you should read this, my dear," she said as she handed it to her. "I've kept it all these years. I've wept many tears over it. The regret and guilt that I didn't contact my precious Lillian remains with me to this day. Maybe reading this will help you understand."

With a lingering scent of violets, her grandmother left the parlor. Even before she opened the envelope, Laurel knew who had written the letter. By the light from the fireplace she read,

Dearest Mother and Father,

By the time you read this, Paul and I will be a long way from Boston. We were married by a justice of the peace at the courthouse a few days ago. It was not the church wedding I've always dreamed about, but Paul is the man I love. It breaks my heart to have to choose between you and Paul. I would rather have had your approval and blessing. I love you both dearly and never wanted to hurt you in any way. I hope there will come a time when you will forgive me.

Your loving Lillian

Laurel was not sure what awakened her the next morning. Perhaps it was the snip-snip of the gardener's clippers in the garden just below her bedroom window. Or maybe it was the quietness. She was used to the shouts of drivers in delivery wagons and the voices of other roomers outside her room. This place was very different from Mrs. Sombey's boardinghouse.

As she snuggled in the fragrant lavender sheets, she pulled the satin-covered feather quilt up closer. Her eyes roamed the room, sweeping up through the lacy crocheted canopy of the dark mahogany four-poster bed to the little desk between the two windows. This was her mama's bedroom! Her mama had slept here, in this very bed. She had played with her dolls and studied her lessons here. In this spot! Laurel felt closer to her mama than she had in years. It was almost as if she were there too.

"Morning, miss." A maid in a ruffled cap and apron suddenly peered in the door. "Just came in to light the fire and warm up the room before you get up." As the young servant walked toward the small, white marble fireplace, she added, "Your grandmother would like you to join her for breakfast."

Laurel smiled. As the room warmed, Laurel reached for the worn envelope lying on the bedside table. She pulled out the fragile, thin sheets of paper to read her mother's letter again.

How very sad, she thought, that anger and misunderstanding can ruin people's lives. How different things would have been if her grandfather had accepted her mother's choice. Her mother had never said a word against Laurel's grandparents. Perhaps if she had lived, she might have told Laurel the truth. Perhaps if she had lived, Laurel's grandmother could have learned to accept the man her daughter had married.

How quickly everything had changed in Laurel's life. She had been in Boston only nine months. She had met Gene and her grandmother. And she was now living in this fine house where her own mother had once played!

As Laurel lay there, she suddenly felt an odd tinge of homesickness. The letter from Ava had blessed her greatly. She wished she could share her joy with her and Papa Lee. For all her new happiness, she missed them and promised herself she would write them again soon.

The first note she wrote, however, was to Gene. Seated at her mama's little desk she told him what had happened. Her pen skimmed over the stationery. "She's very grand, Gene. I can't wait until you meet her. But most of all, I want *her* to meet you."

If Laurel's letters about her new life were enthusiastic, they only reflected her own excitement. One day followed the other in a kind of sunlit splendor. Mrs. Maynard had so much to show Laurel—keepsakes, photos, the portrait of Lillian as a child, even her baby clothes that had been kept in a locked trunk. They spent many happy hours together.

"To lose her was like losing a part of ourselves," her grandmother said as they poured over a scrapbook of Lillian's school days.

Laurel longed to ask why her grandmother had never given her father a chance, but the harmony growing between them was too sweet. She didn't want to break it. There would be time for these hard questions later, after they were better acquainted.

Afternoons were spent in many ways. The two would take a carriage drive or shop in one of the lovely stores or stop for tea at the magnificent hotel where her grandmother had a special table overlooking the park. Here uniformed waiters served them dainty sandwiches, hothouse strawberries dipped in chocolate, or iced petit fours. Sometimes in the evening, Laurel would play the piano while her grandmother read or simply listened.

"You have Lillian's musical talent," Mrs. Maynard sighed. "You must go ahead with your plans to attend the conservatory. I'll take care of all your fees and arrange for a coach."

Laurel began to feel like Cinderella. What would Gene think of these offers? Would her grandmother's generosity extend to him? She would find out soon. She had just received a note. Gene would be home at the end of the week.

Laurel and her grandmother were in the parlor await-ing Gene's expected arrival.

"And where did you meet this young man?" Mrs. May-nard asked, a slight frown puckering her arched brows, her hands busy with needlepoint.

"At the conservatory," Laurel said as she went to look out the window.

"Do light somewhere, child. You're as nervous as a butterfly."

"I'm sorry, Grandmother. It's just that I'm so anxious for the two of you to meet. I know you'll be impressed. And, oh, Grandmother, you should hear him sing!"

"Is he planning a professional career?"

"Yes. He has a glorious tenor voice. He's already been on tour twice."

Mrs. Maynard pursed her lips. "Very few ever actually make it. You realize this, don't you, Laurel? Only the very best."

"I have no doubt Gene will make it. He's determined and he has the talent."

Her grandmother went on. "But does he have the means to finance his training? A family willing to support him?"

Laurel hesitated. In truth, she hadn't met Gene's family and didn't know very much about them. Should she tell her grandmother that they were hardworking Italian fishermen and that Gene was working odd jobs to support himself?

The sound of the knocker echoed through the downstairs. Laurel smiled. It was a bold and confident knock. She started over toward the parlor door.

"Thomas will show your guest in, Laurel," her grandmother said sharply.

Laurel halted, surprised by the reprimand in Elaine's voice.

A minute later there he was. Laurel's heart spun at the sight of him. His skin was bronzed from days on the beach, and he was dressed in a light beige suit and a crisp striped shirt. His hat was tucked under one arm.

Laurel swelled with pride as she reached for his hand and drew him into the parlor.

"Grandmother, I'd like you to meet Gene Michela. Gene, my grandmother, Elaine Maynard."

Elaine held out her hand. Gene walked over and bowed. "A pleasure, Mrs. Maynard." He spoke in a clear strong voice.

"Mr. Michela." Elaine was politely formal. "Please be seated. Laurel tells me you have spent the last couple of months at the Cape."

It was only then that Laurel was conscious of the chill in the room. It was as if someone had opened a door and a winter wind had swept through. Her grandmother's tone was icy and cold.

Thomas brought the tea service in on a round silver tray and set it down on the low table in front of Mrs. Maynard. With great charm, Gene accepted the dainty napkin, flicked it open, and placed it on his knee. He requested lemon instead of cream and accepted one of the tiny triangle watercress sandwiches. Then he answered all of Mrs. Maynard's questions with great ease. Surely her grandmother must be impressed.

"Michela? Is that an Italian name or perhaps Portuguese?" Mrs. Maynard asked at one point. "I understand there is quite a large Portuguese population along the coast. Where did you say you were from? New Bedford?"

Suddenly Laurel snapped to attention. Her grandmother was interrogating Gene! It was as if this had all happened before. Then she remembered. "Lillian, your ancestors came here on the Mayflower, and you want to marry this man with no background!" Her grandmother had told her these were the words Bennett Maynard had spoken to her mother so many years ago. *This* was why her grandfather had never given Paul Vestal a chance! He was from the wrong background. He didn't measure up to the standards the Maynards had set for their daughter. And now Elaine Maynard was taking the same judgmental attitude. Nothing had been forgiven at all. Everything was the same.

Anger ignited within her. How insulting Mrs. Maynard was being in her cool, civilized manner. Laurel glanced toward Gene to see if he was feeling it. But he looked perfectly relaxed, listening to Mrs. Maynard with polite attention. He was the perfect guest.

Gene was not on trial here. Or was he? Quickly she remembered her grandmother's offer to introduce her to some young people "in society." Was this the game? Was she trying to prove that Gene was unsuitable?

Laurel felt as if a smothering cloak had been dropped over her head. This was history repeating itself. Lillian and the unsuitable foreigner, Paul Vestal, all over again. Only this time Mrs. Maynard was trying to come between Laurel and Gene!

Laurel's smile froze on her lips as she sat there holding the delicate handle of her teacup. Like watching a tennis volley, her eyes moved from Gene to her grandmother. She was pleased that Gene remained completely at ease. What a true gentleman he was!

Her heart warmed and melted. Her mother had been brave enough to withstand the pressure and follow her own heart. She would be too. In Gene, Laurel had found more than a pedigree or handsome face and courtly manners. In him, she had found inner goodness and lasting values.

Then Gene was on his feet. "I must be on my way now, Mrs. Maynard. Thank you for allowing me to visit Laurel here and for the honor of meeting her grandmother."

Laurel rose with him. Setting down her cup, she said, "I'll walk you to the door. Excuse us, Grandmother." She slipped her hand through Gene's arm and together they went out of the parlor and into the hall.

"Gene," she whispered. "Can you meet me tomorrow at our old place in the park? We must talk. It's impossible here."

Gene looked at her beautiful face with its rosy cheeks and pretty nose. How he had missed those big brown eyes.

"Yes, of course. I'm working in the morning at the restaurant. How about two tomorrow afternoon?"

Laurel did not return to the parlor but went upstairs to her bedroom. She closed the door and approached the window. Gene's departing figure was already walking down the street to catch the trolley.

"I love you!" She blew a kiss then turned to pull out her suitcase and begin packing.

Laurel arrived at the park the next afternoon, breathless from hurrying. Gene was already waiting. Putting his arm around her waist he led her over to a bench where they sat down.

"What is it?" he asked tenderly.

In as few words as possible, Laurel explained her feelings. "It's almost eerie, Gene. It's starting all over again, just like with Mama." She straightened her straw hat on her head. "My grandmother doesn't even realize what she's doing. I don't want to hurt her, but I can't stay there anymore. I don't want to go back to Mrs. Sombey's, so I must find another place to live."

Gene listened attentively. He waited a moment before speaking. "This is too important a decision to make right away, Laurel," he began slowly. "You've waited too long to find your mother's family—"

"But—"

"Wait, let me finish." He held up his hand. "Your grandmother is old and set in her ways. She's used to managing things, servants, other people's lives. Your leaving won't change her, Laurel. I can see you mean a great deal to her. This has probably given her a new lease on life." Gene took one of her hands in his. "Of course, she's full of plans for you. Just think what her life must have been like all these years before you came. Think what it'll be like if you leave her now."

"But, Gene, she wants me to become something I'm not! And to think I thought my adoptive mother was possessive!"

Gene smiled.

"But what shall I do?"

"I think you should be patient with her, gentle and understanding the way you always are. She'll gradually loosen her grip. I think she's afraid you'll slip out of her hands and that would be like losing her daughter all over again."

Laurel felt the tears coming.

"Don't worry, I'll help you. Together we'll win your grandmother over. I'm sure she doesn't want to make the same terrible mistake twice."

"Yes, I suppose you're right, Gene."

When she sniffled, he whipped a huge white handkerchief out of his pocket to mop her tears. "I have another surprise for you."

Laurel eyed him suspiciously.

"It may be a few weeks before everything is worked out," he added, "but there's a good chance the conservatory is going to hire me as one of their coaches. If that happens, we can get married right away." He looked at her hopefully. "Unless you've changed your mind."

"Of course I haven't changed my mind! This wouldn't mean giving up your singing career, would it? I want your dream to come true."

"Laurel, don't you know by now? You are my dream come true! You inspire me, make me want to succeed even more in my career. This opportunity will provide me with practice time and the chance to study different languages so I can sing opera." He raised her hand and kissed it. "And we would be together."

Gene hesitated and a mischievous look came into his eyes. "I've got more."

"Tell me."

"The owner of the art gallery at the Cape has a gallery here in Boston too. It seems his partner went down to look over the paintings in the shed. Apparently, he became very excited when he found the ones by your father. Anyway, he would like to include your father's work in a show he's planning."

"How wonderful. But—" her sunny smile faded. "I wish it could have happened while my father was living."

"Well, I'm sure he'd be happy to know the daughter he painted will be receiving the benefits."

"What do you mean?"

"The gallery wants you to look at all the paintings and decide which ones you want for yourself. Then the owners will put the others on exhibition and for sale. They'll take care of the expenses of cleaning the canvases, framing, advertising, and, of course, they'll take a percentage of each sale. But from what they tell me, Laurel, you should be a very wealthy young lady."

Laurel stared back at Gene. For so long she had hoped to trace her parents and find her identity, but she had never expected anything like this. Emotion swept over her. Gene took her in his arms and held her while she wept.

24

"But I don't understand, Laurel," Elaine Maynard's expression was a mixture of bewilderment and distress. "Why must you go? I've tried to make you comfortable here. I want to help you through the conservatory."

"I know, Grandmother, and I appreciate all you want to do for me." Laurel sipped her warm tea. "But I have other plans now. Gene has been offered the job so now we can be married."

"But, Laurel, I had it all planned. I wanted you to make your home here with me until you met a suitable young man." Mrs. Maynard shook her gray head. "I wanted to give you a reception and introduce you to society."

Laurel smoothed the blue cloth napkin in her lap.

"It's not that I'm ungrateful, Grandmother, but your plans are not my plans." Laurel spoke with quiet dignity. "I've found the person I love. Gene is everything I want. And we both want you to be a part of our life."

The request touched a chord in the elderly woman's heart. Nothing was as important as this granddaughter. In a way it was like finding the daughter she had lost. Elaine Maynard knew she could not repeat her husband's mistake or she would lose this treasure too.

Years of pain and regret began to seep out of the old woman's soul. At long last, she understood. This was all her daughter had ever wanted, to live happily with the man she truly loved. This was the reason she had left, to follow her heart. Tears of forgiveness trickled down the elderly mother's face.

Laurel got up to walk around the table. Within moments, she was hugging her grandmother. Their tears mingled as their cheeks touched. Yes, all had finally been forgiven at last.

The young couple set the date for November 30, 1901, in Meadowridge. Laurel wrote Dr. Lee and Ava, who were delighted to host the wedding. Mrs. Danby agreed to make the wedding gown, and the Meadowridge Community Church was promptly reserved. Slowly everything was falling into place.

One Saturday evening in October, Thomas was removing the Japanese fan screen in front of the hearth to start a small fire in the parlor fireplace. Laurel had just completed a sonata on the piano while Elaine worked on some needlepoint. Laurel turned toward her grandmother.

"Would you like to attend St. Mark's with me tomorrow, Grandmother? Gene has been hired as a soloist, and you've never heard him sing. We can ask Gertrude and Ormond too."

A shadow crossed Mrs. Maynard's wrinkled face.

"Is something wrong?" Laurel closed the music book.

"It's just that—" Elaine began to fidget with the strand of pearls around her neck. "Your grandfather was so bitter after Lillian left—" She paused. "St. Mark's was our church, Laurel. I haven't been there in a very long time."

That Sunday morning, Elaine Maynard took her place in a special pew identified by a small brass plaque engraved with the name MAYNARD. Looking regal in a gray, fur-trimmed coat, the elegant woman slipped in and sat down beside her granddaughter. Gertrude and Ormond had already arrived.

Elaine had forgotten how magnificent a church St. Mark's was. The stained-glass windows reverberated with each deep full chord from the pipe organ. Her thoughts turned back the hands of time to her precious Lillian. How long it had been since she had sat in this very pew with Lillian and Bennett and listened to this wonderful music. How long it had been since she had given herself permission to pray. Now that her heart had become free from the guilt and shame, she felt free to worship again too. She was grateful.

And then she heard it. The rich full tenor voice resounded through the rafters. It was unlike anything she had heard in a long time. Gene was singing "It Is Well with My Soul."

Tremors coursed through Elaine's fragile body. How blessed I am, she thought. Forgive an old woman her sins, Lord, she prayed. And thank you for bringing Laurel into my life. Thank you for renewing my hope. Yes, Lord, at last it is well with my soul.

Meadowridge

There was not the slightest tinge of sadness in Laurel today. Her step was as light as her heart, her pulse racing with excitement. Clasping her hands tightly together, she moved to the edge of the platform to peer down the tracks. She could already hear the train whistle in the distance.

November was mild in Arkansas this year, and Meadowridge never looked lovelier—neat white frame houses, pleasant curving streets with white picket fences, gardens still boasting purple and yellow flowers.

Oh, it was good to be back! Laurel's reunion with Papa Lee and Mother had been wonderful. Ella had been cooking all of her favorite foods. Mr. Fordyce had visited. She had learned that Dan was studying hard and doing well in medical school. She had even gone out to visit Kit, who was caring for Cora Hansen at their farm. There, she had learned that Toddy was still in Europe with the Hales. For a moment, the disappointment that her dear friend would not be at her wedding cast a shadow on her happiness. She missed Toddy and prayed that they would meet one day again soon.

The bride-to-be had spent more than one afternoon swinging on the front porch and many evenings sharing her joy with her parents since her return. Mrs. Danby had just finished her beautiful beaded wedding gown, now hanging in her closet. Ella had been cooking for days, eager to make a good impression on "Mr. Gene," while Jenny had been busily polishing and cleaning until the house sparkled.

Another train whistle sounded in the distance. Standing beside the yellow frame Meadowridge station brought back many memories for Laurel. The day when she and the other orphans had arrived on the Orphan Train. Then the misty day she had left Meadowridge to go to Boston, not sure she would ever come back. Now eleven months later, here she stood on the same platform getting ready to meet the man she was going to marry. Life couldn't be more wonderful.

The train rounded the bend and screeched to a stop, steam hissing and the grinding noise of steel against steel. She searched the passengers getting off until she saw him. "Gene! Gene!" she called, waving her hand.

Gene swung down from the high train steps. At last! There she was!

"Oh, Laurel, I've missed you so!" He caught her up in his arms.

Laurel quickly gave directions to the baggage clerk to have Gene's luggage sent to the Meadowridge Inn, where Dr. Woodward had made reservations for him.

"The house isn't far, so I thought we'd walk," she began as she slipped her arm through his. "I want to show you everything."

As they strolled hand in hand, Laurel realized she was seeing things through Gene's eyes. They crossed the bridge leading to Main Street then turned onto a winding lane with tall, arching trees. Laurel pointed to a white frame house with green shutters at the end, a bunch of colorful Indian corn tied with wide yellow satin ribbon hanging on the front door.

"There it is." She smiled. "Come on."

As they went up the porch steps, the door opened and Dr. and Mrs. Woodward greeted them.

"Gene! How wonderful to meet you at last," Ava said warmly.

"Welcome . . . son." Dr. Woodward smiled, shaking the young man's hand.

Promptly at four, Ella served dinner. Jenny had come to help and could not seem to stop smiling as she waited on them. Each time she caught Laurel's eye, she gave her a solemn wink.

Everything was perfect. Ava had arranged the table with a fruit and flower centerpiece of grapes, pears, and purple asters mixed with marigolds. She had also brought out her best Devonshire lace and linen table-cloth and napkins. Polished silver glistened beside the delicate crystal goblets.

Ella had outdone her best. The golden brown turkey was moist and tender. Melted butter pooled in the middle of mounds of snowy-white mashed potatoes. Creamed peas and pearl onions, warm gravy, pickles, peach chutney, and, of course, cranberry-orange relish completed the fare.

Dr. Woodward sat at the head of the table with Laurel on his left and Gene on his right.

"Let us give thanks," he said, holding out his hands.

"Most gracious Father, we are more aware than ever of the many blessings you bestow on us. Thank you for our daughter, Laurel, and for the fine young man who will be her husband and our son. Thank you for the blessings of health, food, and shelter. We ask to be led by you in all things. In Jesus' name, Amen."

Ava suggested they wait until later to have some of Ella's choice desserts, pumpkin, apple, or pecan pie, and, of course, Laurel's favorite, custard pudding. So, taking their coffee, the four of them went into the parlor.

The curtains were drawn and lamps lit. Dr. Lee put a match to the fire that he had prepared earlier. The kindling caught immediately with little snapping sounds, sending up spurts of bright flame. Soon a nicely burning fire glowed brightly in the hearth, reflecting on the brass fender and andirons.

"Why don't you play for us, dear?" Ava suggested.

Laurel took her place at the baby grand. For a few minutes her fingers roamed the keyboard as if trying to find the right melody for this special time. As she began, memories came flooding back of the first time she had seen this room and discovered the piano. She played on, going from one song to another. As her fingers moved across the keys, her mind wandered back and forth, everything coming together, past and present. All of her experiences were taking shape, fitting into a whole.

All at once, Laurel knew the joy of coming home. She had been on a lifelong journey to find her "real" family. Although she would always cherish the heart-shaped locket still hanging around her neck, for the first time she realized that her dream had come true. God had given her more than one family and one home. He had been with her wherever she went. Sitting here at the piano in the warmth of this familiar room, Laurel Maynard Vestal realized she was no longer an orphan. She was a lost child who had finally come home.

About the Author

I grew up in a small Southern town, in a home of story-tellers and readers, where authors were admired and books were treasured and discussed. When I was nine years old, an accident confined me to bed. As my body healed, I spent hours at a time making up stories for my paper dolls to act out. That is when I began to write stories.

As a young woman, three books had an enormous impact on me: *Magnificent Obsession, The Robe,* and *Christy.* From these novels I learned that stories held the possibility of changing lives. I wanted to learn to write books with unforgettable characters who faced choices and challenges and were so real that they lingered in readers' minds long after they finished the book.

The Orphan Train West for Young Adults series is especially dear to my heart. I first heard about these orphans when I read an *American Heritage* magazine story titled "The Children's Migration." The article told of the orphan trains taking more than 250,000 abandoned children cross country to be placed in rural homes. I knew I had to write some of their stories. Toddy, Laurel, Kit, Ivy and Allison, and April and May are all special to me. I hope you will grow to love them as much as I do.

Jane Peart lives in Fortuna, California, with her husband, Ray.

The Orphan Train West for Young Adults Series

They seek love with new families . . . and turn to God to find ultimate happiness.

The Orphan Train West for Young Adults series provides a glimpse into a fascinating and little-known chapter of American history. Based on the actual history of hundreds of orphans brought by train to be adopted by families in America's heartland, this delightful series will capture your heart and imagination.

Popular author Jane Peart brings the past to life with these heartwarming novels set in the 1800s, which trace the lives of courageous young girls who are searching for fresh beginnings and loving families. As the girls search for their purpose in life, they find strength in God's unconditional love.

Follow the girls' stories as they pursue their dreams, find love, grow in their faith, and move beyond the sorrows of the past.

Look for the other books in the Orphan Train West for Young Adults series!

TODDY

Left at Boston's Greystone Orphanage by her actress mother, exuberant Toddy sets out on the Orphan Train along with her two friends, Kit and Laurel. On the way, the three make a pact to stay "forever friends." When they reach the town of Meadowridge, Toddy joins the household of Olivia Hale, a wealthy widow who wants a companion for her delicate granddaughter, Helene. Before long, Toddy wins their hearts and brightens their home with her optimism and zest for life.

As the years pass, Toddy brings much joy to Helene and Mrs. Hale. Yet happiness eludes her. Is Toddy's yearning for a home only a dream?

KIT

JANE PEART

Kit

Orphan Train West
SERIES

After her grieving, widowed father leaves Kit, her younger brother, and her baby sister at Greystone Orphanage in Boston, Kit wants desperately to bring the family back together. But the younger children are adopted and Kit is sent West on the Orphan Train. Along the way, she and her friends, Toddy and Laurel, make a pact to be "forever friends." At the end of their journey, they each go to live with different families in the town of Meadowridge.

Kit is taken by the Hansens, a farm family who wants to adopt a girl to help the weary mother of five boys. Kit rises above her dreary situation by excelling in her schoolwork. But will she ever realize her secret longings to love and be loved?

IVY & ALLISON

Ivy Austin dreams about being adopted and leaving the orphanage, but when her life takes a strange turn, she ends up on the Orphan Train. There she meets Allison, whose pretty features and charm are sure to win her a new home. Worried that she will be overlooked by potential parents and not wanting to be left behind, Ivy acts impulsively.

As Ivy and Allison grow up together in the town of Brookdale, their past as insecure orphans still hurts, even though they have loving adoptive families. Their special friendship is a comfort, but is it strong enough to withstand the t Ivy's secret?

JANE PEART

Ivy & Allison

Orphan Train West
SERIES

Coming soon!
Book 5 in the
Orphan Train We
for Young Adults s
April and M